CW01066461

L.2f

ALBERT RIDES
AGAIN

by Jack Trevor Story:

Novels

The Trouble With Harry
Protection For A Lady
Green To Pagan Street
The Money Goes Round and Round
Mix Me A Person
Man Pinches Bottom
Live Now Pay Later
Something For Nothing
The Urban District Lover
I Sit In Hanger Lane
Dishonourable Member
One Last Mad Embrace
Hitler Needs You
Little Dog's Day
A Company of Bandits
The Season Of The Skylark
The Blonde and the Boodle
The Wind In The Snottygobble Tree
Crying Makes Your Nose Run
Morag's Flying Circus
Up River

Collections

Letters To An Intimate Stranger
Jack On The Box

Autobiography

Dwarf Goes To Oxford

ALBERT RIDES AGAIN

JACK TREVOR STORY

ALLISON & BUSBY

An Allison & Busby book
Published in 1990 by
W. H. Allen & Co. Plc
26 Grand Union Center
338 Ladbroke Grove
London W10 5AH

Printed in Great Britain by
Bookcraft Ltd, Midsomer Norton, Avon

ISBN 0 85031 996 X

For Evelyn, Ross, Janice,
Maggie and Elaine, dead and alive.

ALBERT RIDES AGAIN

1

'We wore very startly smarched coats and aprons,' he said. Then he said, 'Is there a disease that starts like that?' Getting your words wrong, he meant. She said, 'I worked in a sausage factory. You had to have your hair up. Lot of baldies, surgical caps, wash hands, then all these dicks going through your hands, nip, nip, nip. You had to get your length right and twist them into bunches. It's not meat.' He said, 'Do you want this, then?' She laughed and began pulling it in milking fashion, her little finger trailing to stroke his scrotum. 'We had to pay our own laundry,' he said. It always goes in threes, he thought.

'Why do you always say wife?' she said. 'When you're coming. Wife, wife, wife, wife, wife – '

'That's right,' he told her, 'keep it up, you're getting the hang of it.' He felt that he would not maintain an erection unless it was made legal in some way. Anything fantastic like sex or the pools or a really perfect con trick always seemed to find an escape route. I love you and I want to marry you, darling, he thought. 'Did you say something?' No. Wife, wife, wife.

The ideal thing is to marry a rich but easy lay.

'Either they're rich or they're easy,' he said.

'Who are?'

'You never get both.'

'I'm fairly rich,' she said. And she was fairly easy. It's not the same. 'Did you have anything to do with the death of my husband?' she asked him.

'No.'

'Somebody's putting flowers on his grave,' she said.

Multiple sclerosis starts with loss of word control, he thought, her mention of death focusing him again. She was his boss and they always talked like this. They made love on an undelivered mattress in the Finbow Mercedes trade van. They did not want to commit themselves to your place or mine. But she knew that Marchmont did not have anybody else in the van. He had hung a picture on the wall.

'I've had the police in,' said Kathleen.

'Pardon?'

'That fraud squad inspector – Gamble.'

'Oh.'

'It's about that woman killing herself – what made her do it – '

'Just a minute, love. Have we finished then? I mean it's still in soak.'

'Oh, I'm sorry.'

'That's all right – we've been together now for forty years. Here, use this – I've got to wash 'em.'

'You do it for me.'

Watching his head as he wiped her she ran a finger

into his ear, spidered her fingers across his eyes, spoke lovingly, 'Why do you change the subject when I mention Midge Hammond?'

'You know why.'

'Albert. . .' They made love again. Albert was somebody she once knew. Marchmont was Albert again.

In the shop she called him Marchmont and he called her Kathleen or, with customers present, Mrs Finbow. They had come together without appearing to do so. It all took place in Hitchin, in Hertfordshire. Marchmont was already a character when she first noticed him. He looked like Pinnochio, skinny, flexible, a clown smile instantly frozen into comic stern. His eyes were sooted into his face and his lashes were irresistible, his eyebrows he used as props. His job was agent poling, sticking 'for sale' flags in front of houses and taking them away. Inside his head he was a film star, comedian, singer, whistler, secret agent. Most of the gazumping in Hitchin and district started with a word from Marchmont. He had been to prison once.

'He stabbed his girl friend,' was said about him.

It was first said about him to Kathleen by her husband, Eric, rather proudly. Eric and Kathleen had been on the halls, quite well-known as dancers. In the afterlife of proper jobs Eric would cheer her up by shedding light on the daily round.

'Did she die?'

'No. They were living together. He found her in bed with a chap.' This interested Kathleen and when next she saw Marchmont, driving his Vauxhall or

3

pushing 'for sale' notices into little front gardens, she returned his smile. You could not but help returning Marchmont's smile, which was instantly trusting and vulnerable and sad. It contained the tears of rejection.

In the shop therefore Marchmont was liked by some and disliked by others. Girls found him exciting or funny or frightening. If they were small he would pick them up and cry 'Put me down!' This can be ever so funny – or not. Sometimes he would retail his plan to rebuild Apollo 8 and give children rides to the moon. Marchmont was full of schemes to make himself a millionaire and benefit society. There was bounty hunters, by which anyone spotting a pensioner shop-lifting would get a discount and a conscience. These were the metaphysical elements, explained over a cup of tea and a rock cake, which upset people like Gloria. Then she got used to him and she stayed on.

'Tell us about stereophonic barking dogs, Marchmont!'

People who mastered him, benefited.

'I like the idea of hangouts,' Kathleen told her staff, one morning in May. Hangouts took the capital letter. 'Would you put some money in?' asked her senior salesman.

'No.'

'Ah, good – I can be frank, then.' And to the others, Browning and Gloria and Ruby were there and no customers, he explained Hangouts. Marchmont's conception was to bring street bars to England and get rid of pissy pubs. In Rome or Brussels or Madrid and in New York, you did not need a car to get a drink, you did not need to leave your family at

4

home to drink, you did not have to spend a lot of money or put up with bores or become isolated from home and the things and people that you love. You all strolled along to your favourite or wickedest or whatever street bar, Sam or Joe or Bill or Queenie.

'And you don't buy any drinks!' cried Kathleen, impatient to hit the nub. 'Tell them, Marchmont!'

'You don't buy any drinks,' said Marchmont. And when a customer came in, he told her: 'You ought to listen to this, madam. Keep your marriage intact.'

Often he would sing and yodel, I remember you-hoooo! His impersonation of Frank Ifield and his Bing Crosby fluted whistle and his Spanish maracas – made like a cicada in his throat – accompanying professional fandangos, delighted many people, but not all. Browning viewed him as a fake; therefore Marchmont needed the Brownings in their suits.

'We have to get on, Mr Marchmont,' Kathleen would say, if he had gone too far. And unoffended, his face turned to stone, his voice to Sergeant Bilko, he would rap orders to the universe, c'marn! c'marn! c'marn! Left left left left left. All in all, a nice man. Not to everybody. Some people caught in one of his sales traps got the other end of Marchmont.

And only his closest friend would know the secret of that, for even that was comic. Thought out, rehearsed, practised, done first by Walter Matthau.

'Who pays for it, then?'

'You do, madam, but not at bar prices. Also drink is not drink – it doesn't have to be liquor. Family drinks. Do you know how much you pay for a bottle of whisky if you buy it in a pub? In singles and doubles? Two hundred pounds – give or take. You buy it in the supermarket it will cost you a couple of quid. Wine, whatever you like to pay. Give it to Joe! Give it all to Harry! He'll put it in your locker – you or your family go to the Hangout, give Joe your number, he'll know it anyway. Coming up, sir! Generous measures, no wiping the inside of the glass with a wet rag. It's yours anyway – get it? Cheers! Coca-Cola is free. Somebody play the piano! There's Sam, y'know, play it again – walk home, no driving, bit of exercise.'

'How does Joe make a profit?'

'Ha ha ha! How does Joe make a profit! Joe always makes a profit. Don't worry about Joe.'

'Tell her the truth, Marchmont!'

'There is a cover charge, like a social club, a bingo hall – that's all. Also Joe has a stock of this and that for people who empty their mother hubbards. Think of the advantages,' Marchmont lists them on his Pinnochio fingers, 'You can have girl bars and boy bars and smokers bars and mixed bars – music even or silence, think of the decor! A pleasant place – sings – some time, some where, I know that you'll be there . . .'

'When do they start, Mr Marchmont?' Jen is his slave.

Marchmont hands the problem to his boss who smiles at the possibilities, we'll have to educate the town. 'And what's in it for Marchmont?' asked Browning, darkly. One evening he followed him. People called him Browning for this very reason. In the colours of Hitchin Town, this year of the Great Train Robbery, Browning was brown. 'You're one of

6

those men who turns out to be a murderer,' Marchmont explained to him. There was an animosity between them in which Marchmont, the comedian, had all the witty lines. Edward Browning, a harrier, intended to beat him. That evening on his ten-speed Raleigh, head down, bum up, he passed Marchmont three times in ten minutes. The third time Marchmont was coming out of Duke's flower shop in Church Row. He is taking them to Kathleen . . .

The pretence of lovers ignoring each other or being nasty did not fool anybody and certainly not a sportsman. Sport is full of bluffs. Fucking one moment and saying Mr Marchmont the next is the stuff of offices and factories and shops. It's like pretending to freewheel up hill. Browning managed to catch sight of him entering the churchyard with the roses. Roses for the dead?

'Hello, Marchmont!' said the vicar, Arnold Peck.

'Hello, reverend. Can I use your phone?'

'We don't have phones in churches, Marchmont. People would be offended at the bell.'

'I bet! They'd think the whole thing was trickery!'

The vicar laughed at the tally boy. The vicar was just a plump young man really. There was a phone across the graveyard just inside the vicarage entrance. The vicarage was used for young mums' days and social teas for shoppers on Saturdays and market days. 'I'll leave you,' he told Marchmont, who was dialling. 'No, that's all right, I won't be a sec – you'll want to lock up – hello – ' this to the phone.

'My wife is in bed,' said the vicar.

Marchmont turned round as if offered something.

'Are you sure?' Very quick with his jokes and Arnold is laughing as Marchmont gets his connection. 'No, just a minute, vicar, this is serious too – hello, Mrs Finbow? This is Mr Marchmont.'

The vicar stepped back, not for any privy reasons but to acknowledge the act. This was probably Tony Hancock. 'Listen, I want you to come to the church-yard and bring some flowers – it is important. It's to do with your dead husband, Eric. Eric. Eric – that's right – ' Vicar falls back, covering his face. Marchmont is happy, his face funereal. When it comes off it's rich. And it always goes in threes. 'I'll be behind a tree – I'll whistle. Thank you, madam. . .' He whistled, of course.

'I'm being followed by a little prick on a bicycle,' he told Kathleen. When she got there. She was worried at first until she heard his plan and then she was terrified. 'Do you realise I lose the property if I get married within five years?' Marchmont did not realise that. Who would realise that. 'He must have not only loved you deeply,' said Marchmont, 'but knew that he wasn't the only one.'

'That was Albert,' she said. 'I was one of his customers – Eric was his music master.'

'But we're not going to get married, Mrs Finbow.'

'Oh no – I forgot that.'

'Never forget that,' said Marchmont.

His plan was that Browning would see both of them arrive at the churchyard with flowers as an excuse. These were the secret trysts that everybody knew about. 'He's watching us now – don't look round!'

Browning could be seen on the other side of the

historical Hitchin church stone wall, once the site of the Iceni and Boadicea's surrender, mending a puncture, holding up the inner tube and spitting on it.

'He's got his dick in his hand,' Marchmont explained. 'Tomorrow,' he went on, his hand round her bum, 'if questioned or even if not, we will let it be known, surprise surprise, that we met last night in the churchyard! Well I never, Mr Marchmont! Nothing naughty!'

'And you're not going to tonight,' she said.

'Oh gawd – I wish you'd keep me posted.'

'Tell 'em what?' asked Kathleen, holding both their roses to leave his hands free, standing under the historic oak, her back moving against it, historically. Marchmont kissed her and so on and then, practically, 'You were bringing flowers to Eric and me to my mum – '

'But your mother's buried at Luton.'

'No she's not – that's Albert's mum.'

'Oh God!'

'I'm just a fucking substitute, that's what I am.'

'You'll make more money than Albert, my darling. Keep kissing me. Albert was before his time . . .'

When she'd gone and the cyclist had gone and the vicar was up in bed with Boadicea, Marchmont got on with his prior but lesser intentions, copying down names from the gravestones for his new weekly payment order lists. In Kathleen he had all Albert's expertise plus his girlfriend and all accessories – the master's vacuum cleaner spiel made everything in life inclusive and nothing to pay, pay, pay.

'All right, Jacob Patching – that's a nice bit of mossy green marble you've got there. Died when?

9

That's not very nice – died. You die but your wife's laid to rest. That's sexism that is. Here lies the body of Jacob Patching – don't come too close it might be catching – ha ha, eh? All right for some. We'll give you a nice warm electric two-bar Cosy Quick coffin heater – I mean bedroom heater, not a penny to pay unless satisfied! No, you don't have to collect it, Jacob – you might go falling down the ladder! March-mont's personal delivery service, compliments of Finbow's – your individual high street warehouse, wholesale murder – I mean magic – well, it'll have to be, won't it, with you down there. Now, who's your neighbour? Agnes Freebody! Lucky old you – '

'Marchmont!'

Marchmont screamed and leapt aside, covering his head with both hands. 'Come out, come out, wherever you are! Vicar! Don't do that! It's my heart. Drifting through the mist like that – you haven't got any legs! Where's your legs? You've left them upstairs with Boadicea – you've got to be firm, you know. The fact is I'm rehearsing a play, Arnold, Reverend – Okay chaps and girls, come out!'

'Don't waste your breath, Marchmont, they've gone. I heard the gate creak open and it didn't creak shut – I've been waiting for the second creak, like dropping shoes, I'm sure you know that one. Is this a relative, Agnes Freebody? You're not taking rub-bings, are you?'

'No! I don't do that sort of thing on me knees – I'm collecting epitaphs, you know, funny ones, for a book. That's right, for a book. Albert used to write books. That's my girlfriend's ex-boyfriend. Very hard to follow – not that I want to.'

'Quite,' said the vicar, playing his part now. He pointed toward the dry fountain. 'He's over there, isn't he?'

'No, that's Eric. That's her husband. I'm the only survivor.' The Reverend Peck laughed and swung his hassock to leave, he wore nothing else. 'Well, you are quite good news, Marchmont – don't hang around in wet grass though. I await your marriage.'

'I beg your pardon?'

'You'll find it's easier in the end – and don't ask me for a biblical reference, ask my wife.'

'Arnold! Arnold!' cried Marchmont, muffling it with his hand as he followed the jolly padre out of the graveyard, jumping the easy ones. 'I hope you're not up to anything dubious, that's all I want to say.' It was a kind of benediction and Marchmont accepted it as such. They were both bred on the same radio programmes. By the same people. Driving back to Finbow's in the morning, Kathy Kirby sang *The Shadow Of Your Smile* to Marchmont in his Vauxhall. He cried a bit, not certain for whom or what, then said, 'No man is an island, Reverend.' Then he thought, when Jesus saw the city, he wept. But he decided against it. It seemed like a creep, borrowing Albert's borrowed phrases to make Kathleen open her legs. Win her heart was closer. Albert did not swear. Ruthless people go unheralded.

'I've seen him do spastics,' Inspector Gamble said. He was talking about our hero, it would not take long to detect. 'Marchmont offends nobody. The secret is he looks like a clown. We used to have him at smokers when he was with Rumbelows, pole squatting – or down the con club. Marchmont would do a turn.'

'He'll do a stretch if he goes on like this.' This was Proud talking, Gamble's gaffer, no sense of humour. He sat impassive while his fraud squad chief did a soft-shoe shuffle and sang Marchmont's harelip lover song, oh, I'm a harelip man, hwaiting for my harelip hgirl, hoh de hoh de hoh. 'Or he can do the shakes, Parkinson's disease or St Vitus Dance – I've seen him go round Woolworths in the early stages of multiple sclerosis – no offence. With Mrs Finbow for instance – it's rather touching really, sir – ' Gamble saw that he had lost the gamble and stopped shaking. Proud went to the door before blasting the humanitarian with wither.

'One day, Gamble, Gimble I mean, you're going to find yourself in an old people's home – aged forty.' Victoria held the inspector's hand. 'He doesn't understand, Charlie – he's the old school. Hendon is supposed to be modern police, but the college is littered with chaps like Proud. I've got that list – you were absolutely right. All the names are from the graveyard except one – and that was in yesterday's Chronicle because I noticed it myself – Whippenstall. It's whatever catches his fancy, isn't it. He's probably now on the way to St Albans with a van full of dead people's orders – '

'Not too urgent!' They laughed at each other, the inspector and the WPC – Victoria, in fact, Ackroyd, fair, bit pretty, bit plump and sexy, good at neck locks. 'What will he do then? I mean, is it all set up? He couldn't have printed a list, furniture and so on, carpets, clothes, bicycles!' It was his old auctioneering oppos working with him, giving him a church hall for his fly sales. Gamble explained it. He explained Marchmont putting on diseases to go with Albert. All the things that had made Albert Argyle's life tragic, Marchmont memorised. He would trot them out as if not thinking about Albert, as if not thinking about what made Kathleen tender towards him.

'You're making me cry,' Victoria said.

Gamble was going to kiss her but then sat down. He had an idea they were being listened to or watched. In a police station? Bugging was the thing at present, every electrical device was suspect. With this thought in mind he reminded her of their duty. In the lavatory, a glass tumbler pressed to the wall and to his ear, Superintendent Nathan Proud listened, anxiously. His ceaseless prodding at Kathleen's business was really and truthfully, one of his own clichés, to make certain that his police force had not yet discovered Kathleen Finbow's other business. Kathleen had inherited from her crooked and now dead husband, England's first sex shop.

Kathleen Finbow lived in a brothel. Most people do to a greater or lesser extent. They had come together at Bush End in a quite nice house, mostly through the Evening Standard, 3f and one m, plus a stockroom of equipment, a showroom that belonged to the dark side of the business. Kathleen did not invite people home and many don't. When Marchmont got mugged after that evening's fly sale of ripped-off orders, he went to Kathleen's for the first time, for succour. She was not in and that was unfortunate because there was plenty of succour. By the time she got to him he was asleep in her bed and she made the cocoa before waking him.

'I'm sorry I'm late,' she said. A couple of warning phone calls had leaked to her during the night.

'That's all right, matey.'

'What have you done to your fucking head?' she asked him and he shielded his bandaged head with both elbows at her language. 'Sorry,' she said. She was home now and dirty talk was all right. It was a business. 'I'm glad you know about it,' she told him, once she had done the sausage machine bit. 'It's a relief.' It was going to be an easier relationship, more honest. Sex is more earnest and more serious than vacuum cleaners. There is something demeaning about boring things. About concealing piss all.

'They could have killed you.'

'They took about three hundred quid – half mine and half yours.' She said, 'I tell you what – you can lose the lot.' They laughed and they pondered the event. Around them other events were getting pondered. Strangers came and went, taxies hooted, music played and about midnight a woman of forty looked in without knocking, she was naked but in a hurry, giving Marchmont scant acknowledgement, needing equipment. Marchy did not recognise Ruby naked.

'I'm taking one of those things with prickly knobs on the top – okay, Mrs Finbow?'

'Enter it, dear!'

'Will do!'

All laughing mildly at mild and friendly humour.

14

'I found this,' Marchmont told Kathleen, showing her a membership badge.

'What, in my bed?'

'No. At least, not yet. It belongs to the guy who slugged me in the car park – it's a club membership. Some club. They hit you on the head with it – '

'That's Gerry's! That's ever so exclusive – I know it well and so did Albert. He got knocked out there when I was with him, it's in the country.'

'That's nice.'

She laughed and kissed him, held him close. Albert used to say that's nice.

'Does it hurt?'

'Aren't I doing it properly?'

'I mean your head.'

Marchy sat up and groped for a bit of string with his other hand. 'I should get rid of this – it's like period time.' A soft ubiquitous red light lit them. 'I knew something would go wrong,' she said. She'd got her teeth out. She could have got them in again but noticed what he was doing, which was worse than no teeth. 'You're not smoking. That's not a question. It causes multiple sclerosis and that's what gave Charles Bluett his wheelchair.'

'Say that again – where are your teeth?'

'Fuck off, Marchmont.'

It was a touching moment, unrelated to human conversation. Kathleen restored her secret crockery and then raised her right hand and peered into its palm for a moment, stretching her cheeks and then smiling. Marchmont lent down on one elbow and looked at her. 'What's all that?' She explained to him

15

that when women are in a hurry or in bed they pretend their hand is a mirror and it works.

'Of course it works, darling. That's the story of my life. Look at this.' He took out a bit of bridge work. She smiled and said I beat you. And she told him about Albert's girl friend Helen, the dentist's receptionist in Welwyn who got to her while she was unconscious by shouting fire.

'Did Albert know about that?'

'It was his idea.'

'And this is the great man I'm trying to live *up* to? Hero of the never never, the golden age of hearthside tongs and bedroom clocks? Door-to-door knock knock Albert Argyle, Don Juan of the slipping mums, live now pay later, it's all on the never never, cuckoo eggs all over fucking Luton!'

'He never said fuck,' Kathleen told him.

'That is their secret, the canon of respectability, the aspidistra flying, screw their arse off but never say fuck – What are you doing?'

'I'm putting my knickers on.'

Marchmont watched her. 'Can I have a fag?'

It was all over.

Marchmont put out his cigarette quite quickly, though aware that she would use any disease he had caught from the same alarms and excursions among our science correspondents from Baltimore to Bitlis. It's a woman's world whatever they say to contradict it. Anything that isn't romantic, kills you.

'Tell me about your teeth,' Marchmont said.

Because he knew Albert so well that he knew Kathleen and Tres and Alice – she was a Finbow – and all the nuances of the Callendar Emporium story.

16

Albert would not have somebody's teeth taken out. Note the phraseology, mutually understood. *It was his idea*. Albert's ideas were legend. They never worked. Never. And if they appeared to, the harder they hit him when they ricocheted. And Albert Argyle was never toothless. He died making a noise like a pheasant – this is what he did well. Bird noises, clicking his teeth, yodelling like Frank Ifield, singing like Elvis, though only Heartbreak Hotel, I found a new place to dwell, conjuring, telling jokes, selling useful baubles of the age. He was shot dead pretending to be a bird guarding a pile of his own shit which happened to have his name and address on it – he had used an old envelope when caught short up in the woods.

'Albert's trouble was, he had no scruples,' Marchmont would remind Kathleen. Callendar's Emporium had no scruples, but the Finbow Warehouse had scruples. Thus would they reassure each other, soon together again, even toothless. And what an honest-John gimmick that is, in the business.

'He rescued Treasure from those yobboes at the party while reclaiming goods – '

'Damaged goods – she had been multiple raped already and what for? Repossession of a thirty-bob guitar – money first while she's on her back with five skiffle players – '

'What about Mrs Corby's last words?'

'Very inventive,' Marchmont would admit, as Albert once said to the bailiff who likened a distress warrant with putting your foot through a kid's doll's house, very poetic. 'It was Reginald Corby's teeth he was after,' Kathleen reminded him. Marchmont did not need it, this old history. What did it add up to? Corby was still at the town hall and Joyce was under a motor, under the grass, driven to it, driven to it, said Albert, to the press, to the coroner, to his mum – but only in his head. He came out of it winning again, in his way.

'Joyce got behind with her payments and started putting it around,' Marchmont said. 'Is that what you've got here, Kathy? Is that why old Gamble comes round? Is this the books we don't see? The sausage factory?' Albert invented that.

'Oh no! Please! It's all innocent! I can't stand it! I want to be wicked. I've decided! Let me be wicked, Kathleen, Mrs Finbow – '

'He used to say – listen – it was one of his turn-ons, he used to say, kind of joke, man shaving and his little daughter runs in from school and says daddy, I've been molested –

'MMM?'

'What's that mean?' Marchmont asked.

'He's shaving. He can't talk. She says this man dragged her into the field and took my pinafore off, then he took my dress off and then – Albert makes it last a week and then dad takes his razor down, he's cut himself – what are you trying to do? Give me the horn?'

'I've heard it.'

'Albert started it. And he called all rubbish saus-ages – any mass-produced rubbish. Not to be sneezed at though. They do slip through your fingers and you do have to nip them, gently, gently . . .'

'Don't come here again,' Kathleen told him over a good pancake breakfast and the seven-o'clock news.

18

This was not an admonishment.

'I prefer the van,' Marchmont said.

'I do, Claude.'

'Mmm?'

'I understand why you prefer Marchmont. Albert's name was Harris. Also, I am being watched – for another year. I want you to leave the house with Ruby.'

'Perhaps Ruby's watching you?'

'No, she's not. Ruby has got her own problems.'

'I don't believe people watch people,' Marchmont said. 'I'm surprised at you.'

Kathleen smiled at him, beguilingly. 'It's the Irish – Kathleen Ryan?'

'*Odd Man Out* with James Mason – '

'And? And?'

'Captain Boycott – wait a minute – '

'I don't remember either.'

'You do look like Kathleen Ryan – lovely. She was my sweetheart before Patricia Roc.'

'Kathleen had a drink problem – we're related.'

'What about her teeth?'

'I never kissed her,' Kathy admitted and then heard feet on the stairs and ran out of the room, leaving the door open. Marchmont got ready to leave, wiped his mouth with the back of his hand, felt his body, tenderly for strains, looked at himself in the palm of his hand, something old, something new. The front door closed and Albert watched a man the length of the front garden path.

'She can't do it.' Kathleen returned looking fraught. 'She had to go out.'

'Who's the bloke?'

'Oh – ' she glanced at the window – 'That was Ruby.'

'She had long hair last night.'

'That was a wig.'

'She's a man, then?'

'No. She's bald – it was all cut off by the RAF – not the RAF – IRA – we've got to start moving, Marchy – ' Marchmont made his mock bewildered face, his Yogi Bear blink.

'What, the bombers?'

'Shits, killers, murderers, child dismemberers – they don't speak for the Irish, not for me, not for my family. My brother Pete was shot when he was jogging – through Ardmore, the film studio, he was an electrician – they always get the wrong man, they're Irish, you get a revolution and they kick in the wrong goal – '

'Was he killed? Your brother?'

'No – he wasn't even killed.'

They both laughed briefly; briefly because of an explosion as soft as thunder but shaking the table china so that the end of a pancake fell on the carpet, maple syrup down. Marchmont said: 'They must have heard us . . .' Kathleen, shaken, held her chief salesman for a moment, then sat him down to link her legs around him and relax into his lap. She told him about Ruby.

'They called her The Maid of Bective Bridge. She was a heroine at seventeen, in love with an English soldier. One night in December, blowing freezing cold rain and dark as pitch, the republican army mined the bridge to blow up the first unit to cross it – they knew exactly when it was coming from the

20

village hairdresser. The girls got themselves up for their sweethearts and Ruby was one of those except by sheer luck she heard Michael's voice on the radio, picked up by her hair dryer, d'you see.' Marchmont kissed her and soothed her. She was sounding Irish, which she was.

'What did she do?'

'Ah, it was a brave thing – and her frightened of cows, as we all are – she let a whole field full of the beasts wander out and blow themselves to pieces just before the army truck arrived – she was seen soaking wet and freezing and hiding in the bushes! Shots were fired from both sides, each thinking it was the other attacking. A week later she was disappeared. Nobody expected to see her again. Though I would myself, Marchmont. The republicans are men and women of our blood and recognise true heroism and wit – particularly wit. It was a very witty thing.'

'That it was,' said Marchmont.

'She came to England pregnant, but they never let hold of her. She had the obligation, d'you see. They put her first here and then there – she worked in the nursing home where the royal baby was born.' Marchmont could hardly believe such a thing was possible. 'And then, d'you know what? D'you know the Cliveden house? The Astors' place for god's sake – Ruby was at Cliveden through all the comings and goings of the Foreign Office and Russian spies and the like, not to mention the girls – well, she did a bit of it herself and that always gets you out of an obligation. They've been looking for her ever since, mind – that's why she rushed out just now. She had word. Did you hear her phone go at about five this morning? Nor did I, dear.'

'Wife,' said Claude. 'Wife, wife, wife.' They went back to bed for half an hour.

2

Marchmont's blue Vauxhall had been blown up. As they came up to it, the playing children already pinching everything shiny, the salesman was saying, 'And what happened to Ruby's baby? Was it all right?' The baby was fine and well cared-for in a house full of women, most of them on the game. 'There he is – Roger! Have you had your breakfast? He was named after Sir Roger Casement, shot by the English for spying for us – I mean for – '

'I know what you mean, love – where's my car?'

'Was it a blue one, mister?'

It came together – not the car – very slowly and painfully. Bush End in Hitchin is the kind of builder's speculation that reaches out on unmade roads through partially cleared demolition often mistaken for parking space.

'There's Ruby's blue Vauxhall,' Kathleen said, pointing. 'When she's a man she drives a little white Fiat 5. She must have used that this morning – ' They were both in shock. Marchmont was wearing a milkman's smock. In view of the Ruby story it seemed clear that the IRA had made another blunder. 'But who set off the bomb – somebody must have got in my car.' There was something over there in the spinney; it was the road sweeper and he was not quite dead.

'He's breathing,' Marchmont said.

'Go through his pockets,' said Kathleen. She had found the watcher. Roger Quiggley aged four stood with his winkle in his hand, peeing on a bird's egg, for it was May. Up came a police car as Marchmont was pocketing the contents of the unconscious man's wallet but leaving the notebook. Two bobbies, both strangers to Marchmont, both in love with Kathleen first. Are you all right, madam? Do you know anything about this, sir? They sorted it out and an ambulance arrived. Nobody arriving seemed to know that whatever had happened it had happened an hour and a half ago. If he had not been alive, Marchmont thought, about the corpse, he would have been dead. In the middle of the muddled activity the little private detective and credit agent, for that is what he is, sat up and looked around. 'Where am I?'

'You got blown up, mate,' Marchmont told him.

Five policemen now looked round. The early sergeant said: 'I didn't know that, sir?'

'I'll see you at the shop, Marchmont!' Kathleen Finbow had suddenly seen police chief Proud entering her house carrying flowers. Marchmont watched them and drifted off. 'Just a minute, sir – are you the milkman? Sir!' Marchmont drifted back and joined the activity, afterwards getting a police lift back into

24

town. He would have to use the shop van until the insurance coughed up.

'Morning Mrs Finbow! Sorry I'm late. I had a bit of a heavy old do this morning. My car's crooked up – anything happened?'

'You take it easy, Marchmont,' Kathleen told him. Then she called to their little yiddish shop boy: 'Gringo! Get Mr Marchmont some tea. Come and sit in the office, Marchy, and tell me about it.' Marchmont followed the boss into her office and took out his findings. 'That's just what I was going to do, madam.'

She looked her prettiest, knowing that he was cross. 'Here you are – take a gander, the secret life of a tally shop queen on six cigarette papers. Writ small . . .' So small she could not read the detective's tiny print. 'Don't bother, darling,' he said, ignoring the entrance of Gringo and suddenly with the coming of love – jealousy. He had read the list, copied it down for his own vengeance file; men she had seen, met, asked in, taken out, screwed in back seats and gone to Paris with. And five women and one pervert, details unknown.

'Don't be mad at me. Please. This is Eric's side of the business – sex aids. It's the new thing and all perfectly legal and therapeutic – everything comes from Miss Oates, of Preston.'

Marchmont just looked at her. It was one of those defences that digs its own destruction. She said: 'I'm a catholic and I wouldn't touch anything pornographic, Marchy. This I can handle but mostly by mail. Eric was just about to open a chain of shops, sex shops, the first in England, when he got drowned. He was fishing, you know. He was going to pick up Gerry Chapman that night and fish off the Hamble, but Gerry couldn't make it and he went alone. The boat turned up empty, fully rigged and loaded with fish.

Eric's body was found and his ankle was red to bleeding by the rope – it must have trapped him and left him hanging over the side. I've never told you before. Do you know why? Because I am always afraid I am talking to the person who did it – that it was part of a collusion? That Gerry put you in here afterwards to kill me too – '

'Please shut up. Can we have one thing at a time?'

'I want you to forget this fucking list.'

The cards were down now.

'He called her darling!' came Gringo's voice, out in the shop. Somebody whistled the Dave Clark tune, *Bits and Pieces*, somebody laughed, a Finbow 24-weeks-to-pay radio came on and a kettle whistled as the defences came crumbling down. Three new customers came in looking for more debt. 'I have a message for you Mr Marchmont.' Marchmont looked round and saw a pretty girl in a green smock up to her knees.

'What's your name?'

'Rosie – I've been here three weeks.'

'Nice to know you – what's the message?'

There was this man in a Jag and his card. Marchmont rang and talked. This is Marchmont at Finbow's. 'I like that,' said Kathleen. Marchy put his fingers on her lips which delighted Rosie – others came to listen.

'Marchmont listen – you're getting big. You've

been mugged and bombed – that's big. Come and see me. I have underrated you. We'll do some business. Bring Kathleen – ciao!'

'Who was it?' Kathleen asked.

It was Gerry Chapman at Gerry's in the Country. 'Keep breathing deeply, like this,' Kathleen told Marchy. He was shaking. She was pleased to see his wet fish condition compared with Albert's insufferable one-upmanship. In The White Rabbit it was well known that in The Gerry Chapman Story Gerry had worked as a torturer of SOE agents at Gestapo headquarters in the Avenue Foch. Pushing them into baths of cold water and pulling them out, watched by fraulein typists. He was a double agent, Kathleen would explain.

'When he was caught he was a double agent,' Marchmont said.

'He's got a nice car,' said Gringo. 'Is he a director, Mrs Finbow.' Sleeping partner, Marchy thought. To avoid the point Kathleen asked Gringo about his name. 'It's what my dad calls me. My step-dad, Gonzales – it's because I'm white.'

Rosie said: 'It's because he likes you.' 'They all laughed – at Christopher Colombus, when he said the world was round!' Astonished, they looked at Browning who had sung as a critical comment on the laughing, while he was working, issuing shop orders for tomorrow.

'Brown dog barks,' said Marchmont.

'Where did you find Jacob Patching, Mr Marchmont? And how are yesterday's gravestone masons spelling Whippenstall?'

'Gringo – go and let his bicycle tyres down.'

'I want you all here,' said Kathleen. She had let down her hair and was combing it, resting back on the Finbow Comfy Telly Chair. 'Marchmont's car has been blown up.'

'Where's Ruby?' asked Rosie, not wishing her best friend in the shop to miss another story.

'She's gone away,' said Kathleen.

'For another short time,' said Marchmont.

It joined the general light-heartedness of the times. God waiting.

3

Gloria rushed in on her spike heels with a service return, a hair dryer label on a sex aid vibrator which could also curdle eggs. 'It's that blower again,' she said. 'That's right, blame the operator,' said Marchmont. They always come in threes. The undercover trade at Finbow's had fooled him for six months while even the cat knew about it – always getting her spine tickled by the boy. He used to think Gloria was out cold canvassing. She looked too much like a whore to be a whore, as some people look reliable.

'What's happened to Ruby?'

They told her what had happened to Ruby. 'It was just a warning,' Marchmont told them. 'Three more cars and they'll get to hers.' Kathleen shook her hair loose and ran her fingers under her breast and sniffed them, sensually, then said as expert: 'They'll force her into another job now they've found her.'

'Yes, well, you're all stripped to the waist,' Marchy said, 'but there's not enough ackers in prick teasers to support the IRA – what they want is a train robbery. We used to carry five million in old notes on the overnight mail from Liverpool to Euston.'

The Irish rose blinked and looked at her lover, her mouth full of hairpins. 'Did you ever tell Ruby about that?'

'Say again?' He cancelled it, another three for the joke book. One of Marchmont's projects was a joke book, Always In Threes. In each good joke there were always two more good variations. The entrepreneurial idea was to persuade breweries to persuade their pub tenants and managers to collect bar jokes from The Red Lion and The Black Horse and The Trouble With Harry and print them for sale in those pubs – the well known regulars would get their jokes attached to pub posterity until they were all wiped out by Marchmont's street bars.

Rosie said: 'There's a man at the door.'

'Who locked the door? Never lock the door. Not during shop hours. If the police come it looks bad – you must all appear to be busy.' Marchmont took Rosie in his arms and licked her ear – joke lost. It was Sam Kidd from Gerry's Club, uniformed, the name discreetly in gold script on his chauffeur's cap, which was made of black leather.

'I've got a present for Mr Marchmont, sir – from Gerry's in the Country. You had your car blown up – they want you to accept the Rover – there's five thousand miles on the clock, it's taxed and insured in your name and here are the keys, I won't wait, I have another car picking me up – '

'Just a minute, just a minute, I don't believe it, I don't want it – '

But it was there. He had got it. He tried to find a

30

loophole, he was shaking and sweating again at the thought of torture or prison – or worse! What had happened to those five thousand miles? And where was he now? 'What a beautiful car – it's the bull nose One Hundred, I always wanted one of those,' Kathleen cried. 'It's yours!' said Marchy. But the chauffeur gave him the documents.

'These are not valid,' said Marchmont. 'How could you get these without me signing?'

'Mr Chapman had them forged, sir.'

Marchmont sunk his long nose into his bony shoulders and put his thumb in his mouth and closed his eyes. They all laughed including Sam the Leg. 'You must bring him along, Miss Finbow – he's another Albert!' Then he walked away but turned to face them all for a moment with a blessing: 'I wish you well to drive it, sir!'

'Wasn't that nice?' said Gringo.

'Some people have all the luck,' said Brown dog.

Kathleen put her arm round Marchmont and hugged him, unlocked the door of the Rover, closed it with its expensive clunk, once or twice. Gringo kicked a tyre. What about a drive? Now? Take the girls home and put the harrier's bike in the boot. Marchmont refused to budge, stuck his hands deep in his trousers pockets. 'I can only drive little blue Vauxhalls.' But he did it, north out of Hitchin then west over the last tail-end cliff of the east Chilterns range of hills, with their smudgy Boyd and Evans springtime promises.

'I always wanted a white one,' Kathleen said.

There was so much to say there was nothing else.

Gerry's in the Country is no stars up or down on The

31

Spider's Web or the Tollainis' Thatched Barn but it was several moves sideways, nights out for villains and molls and still five minutes from Elstree aerodrome and Le Touquet gambling. 'Now you know why Gerry bought you the car,' Kathleen told Marchmont. 'They tow bangers down to the Danzigers studio and use them for burn-outs – honestly.'

Marchmont nodded, grimly. 'It's your integrity that frightens me.'

'Do you know something, Claude? Kathy Kirby was singing here at Easter? Not Kathy Kirby. Dorothy Squires. Some people – '

'Some people say Kathy Kirby is your double.'

'Yes.'

'You get asked for her autograph.'

'Yes. I give it.'

And they laughed, always in threes. 'I hope Gerry is not in.'

'He might be out robbing a bank.'

This was the mood of the evening. Gerry was not out robbing a bank. Gerry and the Chapman story were ranged around the bar or dining or fucking in a bathroom. 'That's not Helga, is it?' Marchmont said, nervously. She said, 'I told you what happened to Helga – '

'Excuse me,' Gerry said. He had brought them up to the cloak room and a vacant Queen Anne suite if they wanted it for the night, as most of his clients did. Gerry, a very big man who could pretend he was Orson Welles and carry it off, probably the best bit of sharpening stone in Hertfordshire, giving it a Bernard Miles yokel joke twist.

'Quietly in there – try holding the roller towel!'

And to the new arrivals he said: 'That's Bill Montana the film producer and – wait a minute – ' he called down over the blue gilded bannister rails – 'Elizabeth! Elizabeth! I thought so – ' He led them on. 'Make yourselves happy, I'll send a tray up and then come and meet a few very special friends of mine.'

Kathleen said, anxiously, 'Not Chelsea Ted?'

'Who? Oh, that wasn't Chelsea that was Frankie Soil – Sayle, I mean – Ted's in Devon. Don't worry, everybody knows about Marchmont, he is top guest and for your wedding, you know what I'm going to do for your wedding? I'm going to fly you to Rome and have the whole of the Hassler for families and friends, maybe a blessing, hah? Now, you get together – my servants are blind. Well, now.' He went away chuckling like a viscous drain.

'Who's Ted?' Marchmont said.

'It doesn't matter – '

Marchmont brought a gun out of his pocket and put it to her left arm, which seemed less threatening. 'Where did you get that!' He said, 'Chelsea Ted – he tried to kill Albert, didn't he? Yes, he did. He was in love with Helga and slept here with her but then left her pregnant – '

Kathleen took the gun from him and put it into her small heart-shaped silver chain vanity bag, wafting out the scent of violets. Marchmont tried a window – 'I'm going – '

'Come here.' Kathleen held her long-nosed loose-limbed hero; she had dressed him in two shades of scrubbed denim pink in a jacket with shoulder-wide lapels and under it a grey cotton shirt worn back to front to simulate clergy, in the spirit of the times.

'Don't do that – some chap'll come in – Kathleen – Kathleen – no, I don't want it out! Stop it!'

Somebody came in softly and laid a tray of cocktails and canapes on the Queen Anne table and left. 'Is that better?' Wife, wife, wife, wife, said the tally boy. Somebody quietly closed the door and voices and music remained in a hidden speaker, make it easy on yourself and breaking up is so hard to do and I got you, babe . . .

'This is Albert,' said Orson, with his deep chuckle.

'Please don't say that!' Kathleen told him. 'Not even joking – '

'You bastard!' said Chelsea Ted. He had only just been to Marchmont and Kathleen with a brimming bottle of the horse, as they called it in Devon, but now he pushed the bottle into Marchmont's face and knocked him down, then knelt on his throat and tried to get his nose off. 'He's wearing a fucking false nose!' cried Ted, imploring people to understand. Kathleen flung herself onto him and put her fingers in his eyes.

'Hold it – this is the police! Everybody stay like that and don't move.'

'Can she take her fingers out of my fucking eyes!'

Kathleen got up and wiped her fingers on her breasts. She was in a nothing blouse and dirndl skirt which hung into her thighs, her hair down to her shoulders. 'Where joo learn to do that, then?' asked Ted. Everybody got Marchmont up and brushed him down and gave him whatever he wanted. The police, a stocky man who looked it was said by his friends like Barney in The Flintstones, was now playing

34

cards. The resumption of normality was as instant as disturbed jelly. Gerry spoke to Ted, both eating nuts, oddly working class, Queen Anne hoodlums – 'I thought you was still on the moor, Ted?' Chelsea Ted shook his head, trusting nobody. The big one . . .

'What is it, Henley?' It was August, that's all.

Elizabeth came down later and sat with Kathleen, two beautiful women. The clientele of Gerry's were grouped to their interests, mostly money-rooted or property and possessions, boats and cars, some film – Dennis Price was staying at the Barn and Ian Hendry had taken some fishing friends up to Linford for trout. Gerry was converting a sand backwater into fish. 'Are you CID?' Marchmont asked Barney. He had thanked him for intervening but the inspector understood all sides. 'She broke his heart, you know – I saw him through it. Well, we all did. He loved her. Talk about Romeo and Juliet. Only Ted's rough. He bought her a bloody great horse – right in here! To surprise her. Roan, fifteen hands, brown and black – lovely – Gerry! Gerry! That horse! That horse of Ted's – for Helga! Tell him! Tell him!'

The story of Helga and Ted and Albert emerged, once he had had his nose pulled and been half strangled, in romantic fragments. It was a story which did not reflect well on Albert Argyle, the lovable comedian, and this explained why Kathleen had kept mum. Kathleen wanted Marchmont to stick to the bright side of the moon. Chelsea Ted filled him in.

'This is it, Marchmont – what do I call you – Marchy? This is it, Marchy, sorry about your snout,

35

what a whopper! No, it's great – that bloody comedian come in Jack's Caff – you know Jack's Caff? I'm going back, what, two years, Autumn 1961. I had a good thing going, me and Sam the chauffeur and a couple of Kraynes – forged fivers. We go in in uniform and plain, CID, turn over your fivers – '

'Are you on the force, then?'

'What, no! He is, who you were talking to, Barney, detective inspector, but a good'un – he can get facilities. They turn over the fivers and I sign for them with Sam to counter-sign and the boss, that's Jack Watson, big man, caravan site and that, also signing – then we take it. Nice and peaceful. Free supper, sausage, egg and chips. Then I spot this bugger Albert, calls him over – he's with a fucking group, coming back from a gig somewhere. He didn't remember me and worse than that he didn't remember Helga Wertzen – that was her name. I said – You remember her – your girl friend – you know, Gerry's, over South Mymms, last summer, you were engaged to her – he was blank as a cow's arse. Then he said, oh, that butch frau! That butch frau! Butch frau? She was beautiful. And she loved him. Nobody stood a chance. He come in one night – sleeping with her all summer, mind, up waiting in her bed while she was still working and that – screwing on the golf course and in his motor, her always waiting for him to turn up, her face lighting up – Christ, sorry, it breaks me up – he come in one night with some fucking blonde hanging on to him. She went running down the garden, Helga I mean, and tried to chuck herself in the backwater – only it was dry. And he didn't remember her! That butch frau. I took him by the frote, I'm not kidding, I nearly had the real cops in! I told him! That girl went home to Hamburg – Kassel her mum lived, all her family heroes in the war, working on the flying bomb at Peenemunde, medals and that – and she went on the game and finished up with clap and everyfink – oh Christ, I'm sorry, mate – ' Kathleen came over with Elizabeth and they held Chelsea Ted, took him to the arbour for succour. 'You fink girls don't love you but they do . . .'

Marchmont sat down on the floor and rested his face in his hands, deeply moved. He resolved to find the German girl, no matter how long it took, and marry her, have some children, he could see them all at Butlins. His dad lives in Essex.

'Here you are, drink this.' Gerry handed him a glass of pale grey liquid. 'It's sal volatile, like Natalie.' The fire of the breath-taking reagent livened the salesman's brain. He shook his head, like a boxer. 'Ruby phoned,' Gerry said. Then he said, 'Okay?'

'Oh, yeah. Right.'

'She's in Liverpool. We're taking the kid up tomorrow. Nice trip for Liz and my kids.'

'I hope the weather stays up,' Marchmont said. He dare not say a word more in case he got an even more mysterious reply. 'She's on the railway – ' Gerry's continuation made Marchmont jump with nerves. 'In the parcel despatch office – overnight express, night mail. T.P.O.'

'I had some of that,' Marchmont said. 'At Christmas.'

'I know. It'll soon be Christmas for everybody – how's the motor?'

The motor was smashing.

'Did you have a good time, honey?' Kathleen was relaxing back in the Rover, her seat adjusted to put her behind the driver. 'Not very,' he said. She ran her hand round his courting tackle, opened her legs. 'Did you have some oysters?' Marchmont had swallowed two dozen. 'You were very impressive,' she told him, warmly. 'Everybody liked you. Elizabeth asked me if she could make it with you. If I minded.'

Marchmont grunted. Promiscuity was a thing of the past. You fink girls don't love you, but they do . . . Love means something more than dick. 'Gerry asked me to go on his boat – at dawn tomorrow, round the Isle of Wight. He has some kind of smuggling pickup on Hayling Island.'

'I'm glad you turned him down.'

'I didn't turn him down.'

Marchmont pulled into the next dark place and gave her one. The car door opened while they were lying on the back seat, half-dressed. A man with a shaven or bald head looked in, holding the driver's door open. 'You stay there, don't dress, I'm driving – '

'We're not breaking the law!' Marchmont said.

'No, we're going to,' said the intruder.

Kathleen said: 'What are you after?'

'I want the list – '

'What list?' Marchmont said.

'I've got it,' Kathleen said. She opened her little vanity bag and spilled the scent of violets and the gun – 'Is this loaded?' Marchmont nodded, quite frightened, his trousers half discarded. Kathleen shot at the man's head and hit it. He fell back and his friend ran away as Kathleen got out of the car,

Marchmont following. She aimed again and fired at the running figure who yelled in pain. 'This one's dead,' Marchmont said. 'Leave him there and get started. I'll telephone Gerry when we get back.'

The Rover had a slight bumping in the suspension for the rest of the journey. It depressed Marchy, as if compounding his fears. Kathleen laughed at him. 'That was lovely,' she said. He was better in cars and vans. Marchmont lived in a caravan but took her back to the brothel.

'Are you coming in?'

It had been an hour's drive and the body and the bald head took turns with the white lines on the north orbital and the A1 – they killed a fox at Codicote. 'No thanks, ta, mate – see you tomorrow – no, don't do that – ' She only wanted to kiss him. It had sunk into him that her use of the gun brought her closer to Ruby and the Irish war than he had realised that she was. The English are not. She kissed him gently to calm him and mother him. 'Remember this, Marchmont. No woman and no child wants to be the subject of a search for bodies, that line of policemen, the dogs, the hundred angry neighbours – and somebody's child, somebody's wife, raped and dead in a shallow grave. I gave that man and his friend a chance to piss off. Goodnight.'

'I know who it was!' Marchy suddenly knew. Not the shot shaven man but the friend, a little guy with a hat over his eyes. 'It was that little detective – who was blown up with my motor. I know it – he was trying to keep hidden. It was.' Kathleen considered it and it seemed likely that the chap's injuries were mostly shock. 'Ah well, he's got something to write in his little crabbed handwriting on his ciggie papers now – I thought he was working for Gerry, but now I don't. Do you know something I found out from Elizabeth tonight? He marks spiders.'

'Do what?'

'Spiders. House spiders. In the bath, squiggling like leaves in the wind across the floor, taking the corner of your eye – he catches them and puts a little spot of Liz's Tipp-ex on them. The leg or somewhere. So he knows if they come back to see him. D'you know, darling – Gerry is a pussy cat. He didn't kill Eric.'

'Perhaps he only kills flies?'

Kathleen laughed, watching the lovely big white bull-nosed Rover car, the best they ever made, cruising away into the dawn. She noticed that there was a police yellow plastic witch's hat banging against the suspension. Why do women think only women use Tipp-ex, he was thinking, from a past relationship with a feminist. That bump was still there and he covered it with a cassette, and honey I love you, and I want to be near you, if only I could. He switched it off as the police waved him down by the Three Moorhens, a nice pub now standing black and white in road lights. Marchmont did not immediately stop but made it appear it was his concern for anything following – they had to chase him to the entrance to the Hermitage Caravan Park. Here he stopped nicely parked into the edge, dimmed his lights and opened the lovely quiet door. The Rover gave him more confidence even though it was his gun.

'Good evening, Mr March.' They had got his name wrong, a good sign.

'Marchmont – Claude Marchmont. It means, climbs mountains.' Marchmont nodded his head in affirmation, a current American rock trend. The inspector noted the correction in his book and tried to catch up. 'You're the milkman.' The PC examining the Rover's interior for half-consumed bottles and knickers jerked round at this – this was not a milkman. Marchmont patiently filled them in.

'Oh, of course, Finbow. Very nice lady. Sad about her husband – I took her for the identification. He got a rope tied round his ankles. Inadvertently.'

Marchmont no longer had to prove he could stand upright. 'What's the query, Mr Saunders? You're Hilary's husband Tom, aren't you? She's one of my special customers – household goods.' He added the latter, comfortingly. 'How's your Teasmade?' And they had a little relaxed laugh about all on the never-never. Jack Lindsay the socialist writer had written a good novel about it and Horace Spurgeon had come too close to it with his film.

'I'll tell you what's gone missing and you'll know why I'm troubling you, Mr Marchmont. Ten milk churns. Them big ones, fifty-gallons, shiny brass, this tall, narrow at the top, stand on platforms at the end of farm drifts – I wonder they don't get knocked off all the time. I mean for the metal alone – lovely workmanship, chased silver, some of it. These are exhibition pieces! They've gone missing from the agricultural museum down at Stacey – I know you know it because I seen you down there! Bugger me,

41

so I did, now I come to remember. You were sticking labels on or something – August bank holiday time?'

Marchmont laughed at him. 'Once seen never forgotten. That's my nose, Mr Saunders. Your wife pulls my leg about Pinnochio – you know what happened to him. I was pole squatting for Rumbelows – "for sale" signs and that – '

'Course you was,' said the younger officer, recognisably a Saunders. 'Remember dad – Marchmont guzzumped our house for us!'

'Lord bless my soul!' said his father.

'Do you want to come in for a drop of something?' Marchmont invited. 'I've got that author's old caravan, thirty-foot Berkeley, talking about museums. This is where he used to write his stuff – and that's not all!'

It all ended very well about an hour later as the police car moved uncertainly back onto the Stevenage road. 'Don't forget – ten milk churns, shiny as gold, and a little trailer they sit on. I dunno where they hope to flog them in this county.' Marchy promised to keep his eyes open, which he did; and he found them. Once he found they didn't know anything about the murder or his gun or Kathleen's fingerprints it became a bit anti-climactic, but pleasant even so. The radio gave him a bit of Boyd coming back from Ireland empty-handed and then he was asleep, where many dreams had been dreamt.

4

'Now here's a funny thing.'

'Yes, sir?'

Gamble and Ackroyd hard at work on the duty deck. She joined him. 'Get Nathan,' he said. 'I'll do it.' He telephoned. 'Superintendent Proud? You got a minute sir – what? I'm sorry, all right, it'll keep – it's Finbow's – what? Oh good – bring your coffee.' Vicky laughed. 'He always come running for Kathleen!' It was the blown up car at Bush End just hit the reports for magistrates' hearings in Hitchin on Tuesday.

'There's no case there,' Superintendent Proud said when he saw it. 'That was kids. They dropped a firework in the petrol tank.' None of the three of them was satisfied with that. Kids couldn't get fireworks in June – it was now June. The wheels of the law. Nathan Proud said, 'You can scrub that, Jason, that's all taken care of. It belonged to the milkman and he's already got a nice Consul out of it – he's delighted.'

'I expect he is, sir – that Vauxhall belonged to Marchmont. I followed it for a week.'

Proud grew thoughtful. He wore cheekbone side-boards and got mistaken for a rose grower and a Member of Parliament – the rose nursery was just along the Letchworth road and if he drove by he got saluted. I was there that morning, he thought. Kathy had given him some extended french letters. 'That's not all,' said his fraud squad inspector. 'Tom Saunders checked him out on those milk churns – I've got a funny idea they're shifting into the museum war. Finbow's I mean. We've got a six wheel farm wagon and a windmill gone missing in a week and now there's treadle sewing machines turning up on the corporation tip – somebody got scared.'

'I see.' Proud could see a way of taking the heat off his Irish rose. 'You might be right about Finbow's undercover business then, Gamble – antiques!' 'Better than all this!' the plump and pretty WPC declaimed, tossing her hand into the desk top of Finbow coloured brochures, offers. You gets. 'You get a free radio with every washing machine, you get a Wilton woven bedside rug free with your bedroom suite – washing machines, vacuums, lawn mowers, they waste their money on this and the kids live on cornflakes – last week Blind Walter Belsen sent to prison for defaulting on a judgement summons, that bloody knitting machine to try and scrape a living. Blind! You can do it by touch! That's what the tally boy said – it come out in court.'

'That wasn't Finbow's that was Callendar's – whoever took over Cally's Emporium – Solly Cowell.' Charlie Gamble liked Marchmont and knew his good qualities – he was good with kids and did Pinnochio clowning at school Christmas parties, made them

44

laugh, played mock football with their caps. He was delighted with Marchy's new Rover and mentioned it now.

'What's it doing in Billericay?' Vicky said. 'I forgot to tell you – I got a call in, ten o'clock this morning – '

'Was he alone?' Proud could have bitten his tongue off. Police were trained for things like that at least. Vicky hid her smile and they all knew it. 'His dad lives at Billericay,' Charlie Gamble said, semi-officiously. They didn't laugh until Proud had gone out and shut the door. They both knew he was screwing Kathy but they were unaware of the sex aid business in the town, over the counter, the little black plain parcels and Frankenstein kits. Addadicks.

Going to see his father was running away.

'Troubled, son?'

Last time his wandering boy had got cancer but this time it was more positive. Marchy told him about shooting the bald man in his bald head when they were making love in the back of the Rover after the night at Gerry's in the Country, about the gift of the new car and Chelsea Ted trying to strangle him for deserting Helga and thinking he was Albert, trying to pull off his nose. 'I don't look anything like Albert, dad!'

'Wait a minute – I'll just finish this.'

Mr Marchmont was playing the guitar.

'I know this – it's Joan's song, she had her baby in prison, I was about eleven – *Our Day Will Come?* That's nice, you're getting better, dad.'

'I can make it last about an hour now.'

It was Malcolm Marchmont's esoteric gift to Mickey Mouse the pops, his poetry, his painting, while avoiding pretty tunes, pictures and stories, sending up the expected; building scaffolds made of mathematics.

'Mr Marchmont is a surrealist,' the probation officer claimed when the boy was being taken into care for want of a sane parent. 'What does that mean?' he was asked. 'He doesn't wear any socks,' the magistrates were told and they accepted it, also a bit of allotment full of failed seaweed (dope). The mother, Rosamund, was a novelist with thirty-five cats. Joan Nane had come out of prison and worked for Stanley Spencer the mad artist and then L. A. G. Strong the novelist and then the Marchmonts, thanks to the optimum after-care placings of Lionel Trilling the probation officer, himself a struck-off doctor and pederast and part of the colour of the fifties.

'Was the gun loaded when you gave it to her?'

'No! I dunno. I never had it loaded. It's yours, dad, you give it to me when I came of age.'

'Oh, it's that one! That can't be fired. Not unless you bored it out. That was a safety pistol, Claude. She must have had another pistol in her bag. Are you sure he was dead? It doesn't seem credible, the detective just running away and her just kissing you goodnight – the police looking for milk cans. Lucky it was old Tom Saunders and his boy – how's his wife? Rachel give in to me one night. Always easily led.'

'I don't know, dad,' Marchmont kept saying. Marchmont didn't know anything. He was worried to death. Malcolm always helped him, always had. And his mum, the two of them always ready to combine forces, even though they had never lived together for more than a few weeks. They weren't married to each other, but to a number of vague lovers and cross-related visitors. There had been rescue drives to Germany after the beer fests. Malcolm with his surrealist mind and engineering background swiftly took the right bits and dropped them into place.

'You have helped the IRA, let's say the IRA in the person of Gerry Chapman, let's say he is laundering the loot, the Gerry Chapman story again – picked up by the Boche in Jersey when they invaded and used by them, so he says, to spy over here – they made a test drop and waited to see if he would knock on a door and give himself up to the English who would turn out to be German! Nasty!'

'I didn't know that. Did he do it?'

'Course not, he's a villain too. Then let's say your Ruby is reccying a big train robbery on your information – that's why you've got the present, the Rover, treated like a duke.'

'Oh Christ,' Marchmont said.

They were sitting in the Green Man pub now in Billericay and it was half-past one, time for food. 'We'll get some nice Galway prawns from Paul – or smoked salmon and sour cream with a bap?' Marchmont did not feel very hungry. 'What's this list, then, dad? Baldy asked for the list, that's when – '

'I know, I know, drink up, boy. She's got the list – it's the names of the gang. I expect you're on it – there'll be a nice cut for you. You get a good cut for the information and you don't have to slog – have you got any idea of dates? No, don't tell me – I think we're being earwigged.'

'I'll have some prawns . . .' It'll soon be Christmas for all of us, was running through the frightened lad's mind. 'It's nice having somebody to talk to,' his father said. He looked well.

They went through the day's papers in the little reading room of the village library and found home page murders. 'I've got a gypsy girl like this, Claudie boy.' His dad was holding up page one of *Reveille for the Weekend*, lovely tits and pouting mouth. 'I think I've put her in the club – we burnt hands together with a bit of wood. I mean, get to my age you have to suffer – here, it's a plant! I just thought. They give you that nice car, two thousand at least – Gerry'll take it back when they've finished with you – then Kathleen incriminates you. That lay-by. She didn't want fucking, that was arranged.'

'But I could have stopped anywhere.'

'They were following you.'

'Why would Gerry want to get me incriminated?'

'I'll work on it – here, taste this, Aldeburgh beach this morning, full of flavour, ta, Paul, this is my – oh, you know – ' Paul, a disused actor, smiled at Marchmont, looked both ways before saying to Malcolm, 'Joan Nane was in last night celebrating on Pernod.'

'Oh blimey she must be out again – with anybody?'

'A chap from the gaol, Chelmsford, Ernie – told me to give you her love.'

'Oh good, I prefer it like that.' Malcolm and his boy laughing together for a moment and a possible solution triggered perhaps in the script writer's mind by the intrusion of prison. 'Listen – I think I've got it. They're going to need you for something vital – you know the MBT's whatever it is – night sorting, PTO's – they'll have someone on the signals and someone on the points – any telephones on the mail vans? No, I tell you what, I tell you what, they could use the pigeons, they carry baskets of pigeons for releasing . . .' Marchmont always enjoyed his father's surrealism and did not interrupt. It helped him to decide on his own, as fruitful people do. He would cut. While it was still possible. Marchmont decided to abandon the Rover for Kathleen to return to Gerry's in the Country, get a train to London then a coach to Bristol and try to travel steerage on a Fyffe banana boat to the Canaries.

'What are you thinking about, son?'

'Have you seen mum?'

'No. I thought you were seeing her, boy. Your brother's seeing her.'

'Oh.'

'That's what it is.'

With the comforting feeling of not having to worry or entertain guilt or obligation, father and son finished eating, got more drink and put a pound note in the Doctor Barnardos jar to play darts. 'Come again before Christmas – that's a nice treble, now go for seven double-sixteen – hold it! Hold it! Put 'em away.' One of Malcolm's tangential pennies had dropped.

'By Paul! Ta ta all!'

'What is it, dad?'

It was a nice walk back to the farm. 'This chap Ted, Chelsea Ted.' Marchmont nodded. 'Why would he mistake you for Albert? Why would he mistake anybody for Albert? If Albert is the one he hates most he must know what Albert looks like. He must have seen Albert – what's his name again? You don't surely mean Horace's Albert?'

'Yes, Argyle. Albert Argyle – he's a relation of Kathleen's, I think so, his wife's name was Finbow, Alice Finbow – I didn't know them, I was in the bloody coalmine, then in hospital and that – '

'Just listen, sonny. I think he killed him.'

They stopped walking and sat on Billericay stocks, on the green, two chaps, one about fifty-eight, the other about twenty-eight; a plain police car pulled in the parking space in front of the Spar village store and the girl constable got some oranges. 'Who killed who?' Marchmont had a patient tone, used to his scripting dad's scenarios. They made as much sense as his *Mood Indigo. Dedication To Eddie Lang* by Albert Harris.

'Go on, then.'

'Chelsea Ted was in love with the German girl and Albert comes along and lays her and then treats her like rubbish and she goes on the streets and gets clapped up – is she dead? I bet she's dead. You find out – suicide. Yes, I would kill Albert. What? Couldn't even remember her? What did he say?'

'That butch frau.'

'And he hit him?'

'Yes.'

'In Jack's Caff? Four o'clock in the morning? I know it. We shot there one night on an Armchair Thriller – it's murder. I can see it.'

'Then why would he go around strangling other people? Years later? Thinking they're Albert?'

'You work it out, Claudie. Be my guest. You're your father's son, your cowboy mother's maverick.'

'Chelsea Ted doesn't even know Albert's dead!'

Mr Marchmont did that thing of standing up and lifting his shoulders and pointing the clinching finger: 'You got it . . .' Marchmont performed his double-Yogi blink but he *had* got it. 'See what I mean?' said dad. 'You murder somebody then you go round looking for them – clever stuff.'

Marchmont was too soaked in the history of Albert Argyle, too tutored in Albert, up to here with Albert and his endearing ways to accept a new ending immediately. 'It was an accident, dad. I mean it's so believable. Cedric and the boy scouts were on a paper-chase that day over the Hoo – you know Luton. Albert's wiped his bum on his own name and address and gets mistaken for a pheasant – he heard the chap coming, heard the gun, did one of his impersonations. Like I do.' Marchmont demonstrated.

'That's a pigeon.'

'It was very ironic, dad. He'd just lost all his girls and the pet shop, his mother-in-law was screwing him and he had a girl living in the car and Alice had been certified, the kid was autistic, Tres's husband Charles was crippled with multiple sclerosis – after four abortions she had got a baby, had to take his dick out to pee.'

'That was the hand of God, then? Albert makes a noise like a pheasant and God shoots him – don't

51

laugh. Think about it. Who shot him? What double-barrel adult countryman can't tell a pheasant from a music-hall turn?'

Marchmont blew his cheeks out. The police car cruised past them and the girl waved and they waved back. She had orange all over her mouth and lived in St Osyth. 'There goes the old bill,' Mr Marchmont said. Marchmont was quiet all the way back to the farm. He couldn't tell Kathleen. It would be like telling sir Shakespeare was a woman. He mentioned as much to his father before leaving. 'Don't be daft, lad,' Mr Marchmont said. He was playing I get along without you very well, as he knew. Kathleen knew, is what they both knew now and it didn't improve the situation for her head lover. Driving back across Bishops Stortford and skirting Hertford, dinosaurs groped high, bull-dozers scraping the new motor roads, all creation on the sixth day, left statued for the morning shift. All change.

'This is a pick-it-yourself farm,' Mr Marchmont had explained. It was unbelievable, Sunday slaves with their arses in the air picking the strawberries for the rich growers.

'I've been trying to find you all day, Marchy! Where are you?' He had a look round, sodium lights, squads of motor cars in this year's shapes and colours. 'I'm on the M1 – at a services.' Hore Belisha opened it. 'Gerry Chapman wants you to go abroad, darling – come here first.' Will do, he thought. 'I love you,' she said. In a flash of inspired historic adjustment, he knew that it was Kathleen had blown up the cows at Bective Bridge and not Ruby. Kathleen had described it too well – and half her teeth were missing. It gave her credibility and made her attainable.

Driving on, Marchmont decided to keep the car.

5

'What's happened to my Turner?'

It was the same summer evening, coming up to ten o'clock dusk and they were in the big Merc delivery van, on the mattress. She was in green linen, now up round her thighs and looking like a camera bellows. He brought his hand away and sniffed it. 'You been with somebody else – just a minute – Gerry Chapman – just a minute – on his boat! I can smell cockles!' She said: 'Mr Browning must have moved it – it'll be safe, he knows it's yours.' And Marchmont made himself comfortable, kissed her for luck, then stood up and stretched. 'Did you go?'

'I did so – it was cold and a bit rough. We picked up some illegal friends of his. They were three miles off the Nub in a Dutch fishing boat, poor sods. We came back up the Hamble in sunshine, all wearing bikinis and mini-dresses – have you seen the mini-dress, Marchmont? It'll drive you mad – ' 'I've seen it, I've seen it! Oh my God, I didn't know that was a dress! It nearly killed this batsman – I came back through the country lanes and the forest and the zoo, remember the zoo, and there was a cricket game on the reccy at Little Berkhamstead – I parked and had an ice cream, recovering from my dad.'

'It's been a lovely day – Brown dog did your deliveries and little Rosie took a dildo out to I don't know where – ' Marchmont stopped her with his expression. She said, 'I'm sorry, you don't like that, do you?' Marchmont relaxed, giving up, 'If you're supposed to be a woman and you can send children out with parcels for perverts, there's not much between us, is there. My dad wants me to give this job up. He reckons you're going to rob a train and I'll be the fall guy.'

'Really? What will I be?'

'He's working on it.'

'Tell me about the cricket, darling.'

'Were they wogs? On the boat?'

'One wog, two Americans and a lovely Indian girl – I think she was with – well, you don't want to know too much, dad might not like it – don't hit me. Cricket!' Marchmont did that thing of taking up all her lovely red hair and turning it into a rope, then lifting her up by the scalp – 'Here – ' he dropped her because it had reminded him of something. 'Dad got raped by this gang of kids, religious kids, you know after Elaine went he got a lodger, about seventeen, didn't drink tea? Did I tell you?' They told each other everything.

They had tied Malcolm on the bed naked and put fish paste on his cock and then the farm cat and sat watching it come up. 'Jehovah's Witnesses!' Marchmont told her. 'You didn't tell me that.' The old man

had to get his locks changed and borrow a shot gun.
'He didn't even go into her room. He used to call
out, did she want a cup of tea, in the mornings before
she went to work and she never did. She told him
they didn't eat house food. They call it house food.
Anything ordinary. They eat in caffs and live in
motors, old motors. One morning dad had this tray
and tapped the door and said can I come in and she
said yes and he went in but she wouldn't take the tea
so he said, he was cold, only in his shirt and pants,
he said can I come in bed, I'm freezing! So she said
yes, like that, like she didn't drink tea. Malcolm got
in – he'd probably been tossing off for her for weeks,
both alone in the farm every night – and she was
lying there on her back in a little nightie and he went
for her, all places at once, he's not bad.'
   'He gets it from his sons – '
   'You haven't seen George, have you?'
   'Cross my heart! Well, we cross more than that as
you know. What happened?'
   'The game was nearly over and the score was ten
men out and the game to win – suddenly – all right,
she lay there and he had one leg over her and his
hands everywhere but he suddenly noticed she was
motionless!'
   'I like it like that – captive!'
   'Jesus! I never thought of that. Nor did dad. He
was down on her and he looked up at her face and
she was staring at the ceiling with her cross-eyes – a
slight cast in her eye, very fetching, Karen Black? He
said to her – he thought she was in what's that trance
where you stay awake? He said, are you all right?
She didn't answer.'

'What an old idiot! She was waiting for it!'

'He was frightened – he could see the headlines. Her father was a butcher and her mother sales manager for Royal Assurance – though she lived in her boy friend's car with an old blanket and this was her first real home. Dad made it nice for her.'

'I bet he did.'

'Well, he got out fast and after that nothing was said except they got him, first his money, then his car, then him, on the bed with the cat licking his dick and these kids watching – six feet tall some of them, fink and fort.'

'Religion does terrible things, all right.'

'Dad has this image to keep up. He was appointed writer in residence and then on various community arts committees and then nuking and readings and his guitar – he couldn't go to the police. Anyway, he's a magistrate. I mean, they'd really got him.'

'He should have done it – remember Laurence Olivier in *Term of Trial*? In the caravan with – what's her name? But did you do it? Was that the Greek actress or Hermione Baddeley? Anna Magnani? Did you do it? No! You haven't got the guts!'

'Listen, cricket. I'd never seen this before. In the middle of the over this girl gets up off the grass and goes to the ice cream van and she is wearing a tiny dress, like tennis or badminton, right up to her arse – she was not a kid! The batsman looked at her and the bowler didn't – broken nose! Honestly! Poor sod. And this girl coming back with two big cornets! I didn't know it was a dress!' Kathleen laughed at him, she had just bought a gross in all sizes, everybody dressing for tennis for the next ten years and no tennis.

'Are they wearing them for work?'

'I've got one. In London they're wearing micro-dresses – level with the crotch. You need nice legs – and tights. Stockings are out.'

'Show me – no, come on. I mean – God you've got lovely legs, stand up, here, take my hand – '

'There's somebody outside – '

'It's a fox.' They were parked outside the shop in Bute Street but you forgot that, once inside. Kathleen stripped naked and showed him how it would be. 'Knickers first and then tights or a body-stocking – but tights are coming now from Kayser Bonda, they ladder of course. Just to the waist – '

'That will drive us mad! You parade it round the streets and offices and up bus stairs and that – and you can't get at it! I like to go up the leg of your knickers – as though we're not doing it. Sitting on me lap and that – I don't know why I'm telling you. Put it away, love, I've got to get back I need a shit and a bath – ' She laughed and slapped his orchestra, 'Well, I can't compete with that.' They got on with dressing and the chap outside gave them half a minute. Marchmont tucked everything in and zipped up then said: 'What does Fatty Arbuckle want? Where's he sending me? We're not smuggling, are we? I draw the line at heroin – ' This embarrassed the listening policeman who slapped the side of the van and called, clearly but not to alarm.

'Excuse me! Is anybody there? Mrs Finbow? It's me! Sid the policeman!'

'Don't shoot him, eh?' Marchmont said.

58

Kathleen opened the rear door and one of Albert's disciples stood there in the rain, holding his helmet, his long face carved with an apologetic smile. 'This is like old times, Kathleen – if I can call you Kathleen, it's nice to see that Irish smile again! Good evening, Mr Marchmont – something's come up you ought to know about, your van, your caravan, I just got a call.' The policeman stood back to allow the couple to step down and finish dressing. 'There was a light in there earlier on, our chap thought he saw someone there and your car not outside – see what I mean?'

'Yes, thanks – I wonder, look, Kathie, I'd better go – '

'Kathleen.'

'Sorry – Kathleen – '

'Hello, hello, this is Officer Nation – ' They were new, the walkie talkies to the beat men and he liked to use it. To Marchmont he said: 'I'll get my oppo to look in with your permission – he's on his noddy bike – ' Kathleen stopped him. 'Don't do that – it's George. Your brother, Marchmont – he rang and I told him where to find the key.' Marchmont accepted this lie for what it was and the Irish rose turned the moment into something more important, holding Sid's hand and presenting him properly to Albert's official successor. 'This is Albert's best and oldest friend, Marchy – PC Sid Nation. They were at school together.'

'Yes, I know, I read the book – I thought you'd be in Luton though?'

'I couldn't stay there in that town without Albert, sir. I got a transfer. Albert was the spirit of the times, sir, when he had something on everything came to life – there's not a book, is there?' Kathleen laughed. 'That's just a saying – though I'm sure Horace got it all down – ' She was stopped by a stricken look on the constable's face. She said: 'He's not dead, is he?' Sid looked at Marchmont as if for permission to talk confidentially. 'What's happened?' asked Kathleen. Then she said: 'Would you like to come in the shop?' They went in the shop without a search warrant – the first time since she lost her hero. Perhaps Marchmont has got the same sympatica, the appeal to the crooked streak in everybody, especially the law.

Charles was dead. Charles Bluett and his years of paralysed suffering.

Kathleen cried briefly and they waited and she said, 'Poor old Tres – and poor old Charles.' Marchmont felt that he knew all these gone people quite well and he grew very depressed, listening to the outcomes and prognosis in the wake of the tally boy's steaming through the middle decades of Luton's century – something like that. Marchmont was not as succinct. 'Now Horace – that's the author, he had your van, sir, when Albert was his milkman – he's over in Jersey, in St Helier, trying to start a business with Tres. Who's now got a lovely little girl! They send me Tres's photos of the islands.'

'I bet that's Albert's little girl,' Marchmont said.

He had fixed drinks in the office and Kathleen was combing her hair again, which was obsessively habitual when at her desk. 'It could be Albert's, sir – Marchmont? May I call you that – your health, both of you, whatever it is. My wife reckons the timing is right – Tres was with Albert right up to the time he got shot. I saw her at the funeral, Charles Bluett in the wheel chair.' The image was a bit uncomfortable alongside the pregnancy.

'Horace Spurgeon Fenton never had any money,' said Kathleen. 'He knew Eric's cousin Alice.' Marchmont remembered. Albert had made a scene in the library when he found his wife holding hands with the writer. Marchmont mentioned this and then said: 'You met Albert at Tres's wedding with Charles?' Kathleen nodded, sadly. Marchmont said, working it out, 'So you didn't know Albert when he was single and pulling the birds?'

Kathleen put her hand on Marchmont's arm, to calm him. She should never have let him see her missing teeth, he seemed to want to possess her now, body and soul. 'Albert was my tally boy,' she explained. That would have passed but for the constable's discreet cough. Sid clasped the jealous lad's hand, firmly, looked him in the face, 'Any friend of Albert is a friend of the force, sir – goodnight all!' They watched him go with the inevitable Albert phrase from Marchy, see yourself out . . .

'Please don't be cross with me tonight, boyo.'

Her mood was to do with the long promise that was Tres and Albert's life together, the babies they never had and perhaps now one that came late. 'Give me some babies, Marchmont.' He said, 'I will.' It was a phrase from a Scottish play, the fabric of their love. The sad jokes that came in threes.

Driving across Hitchin at midnight two cars boxed him in outside the football ground. Nobody got out of them but a window went down, electrically. An American voice came from the face of a stranger who was not a stranger, it was ugly but friendly. It was Sam Spade, in Marchmont's head full of ghosts. 'Marchmont. Hi.'

'Hi,' said the tally boy in his Rover. This never happened in the Vauxhall.

'Marchmont – you never showed.'

'I only just got the message.'

'Yeah, I know – I like your method. Catch this – ' The man threw a long fat envelope package and it fell into a puddle. Nobody got it and the American said: 'That's a lot of dough – disappear, all rightcher, baby? Don't take Mrs Finbow. Goodnight.' Marchmont said goodnight. He sat until both cars had gone up to the Bedford road and turned north. Marchmont made a quick decision. Swiftly he retrieved the package and made a quick getaway after the cars. For no reason except he was getting impulses, Albert Argyle impulses. Ten miles north they came to Henlow with its tatty crossroads and RAF Henlow straddling east of the main road and a private plane coming in low above the cars and getting lost and then found again in the mirror, tipping to land.

'I'm going to fly, dad,' Marchmont said.

His novelist mother thought she could fly and was again a part-time voluntary patient at Hill End in St Albans. This is what had given Marchmont the idea of circulating the story that he had been in prison for stabbing his girl friend – at five asylums in the past five years he had met his mother's odd friends, all stabbers or stabbed. Nowadays George was the one who visited. George had a leaveable marriage. Eight miles on was Shefford and a turn left and north-west to the huge glittering crown of the Chicksands early warning Russian-watcher, spread across half-a-mile of hill and serviced by a small sealed-in American town. Both cars turned into the entrance road and Marchmont glanced after them and saw the barrier and the guards. He stopped further on and parked in the roadhouse and golf club at Clophill where he had worked as a caddy. The country club was still alight in the bar and he talked his way to a drink, then sat and opened the wad. It contained five hundred pounds in tenners, all new, and a typewritten flimsy page of American paper, handmade. The message was simple.

Marchmont kiddo, if you have followed me back to base then your car is the star of my security guard's rear-viewing movie and you had better fly away and never come back until you are an old man. If you have gone home like a good boy, then check with Gerry tomorrow morning and leave destination unknown, like the rest of the list.

Reiner Wertzen (Col)

Marchmont sat not reading it but looking at it and shaking. 'Are you going to be all right?' A girl from the bar was shutting up, he had worried her. 'Find some tablets in my top pocket,' he told her. She searched his pockets and found nothing like medicine. She brought him a brandy and coffee and she took him to her room. 'My mother and family walked out of Danzig and crossed the border when the Germans invaded Poland,' she told him. He began to relax and listen to her, get outside himself. The family had been betrayed by a gaggle of disturbed geese which they had to catch and strangle. Her husband now played string bass with the Pete Allen band at The Head Of The River in Oxford . . . But the tally boy was asleep. As he slept he connected Helga's name, Wertzen, with the man who had made him shake. In the morning in grey light his bed mate was pretty but seemed to have no breasts, only nipples. This is why she was active all night and hungry for it, he thought. 'What's your name?' he kept asking her. He did not check the Colonel's envelope until he got back to the caravan site and the money had all been taken. He was relieved. It seemed to release him from the whole episode, though his foreskin was painful and puffy and kind of blue. On the door of his Berkeley trailer, with its aluminium front steps and Calor gas cylinder alongside, was a hand-written note or quotation – it had been specially written in lettering style by somebody who fancied themselves, the paper a blue sheet from a Woolworth pad with a head of Christ stuck in the corner.

Whomsoever follows my guide no fears shall come upon him neither shall he grieve.

'Tell my cock,' he said.

Whomsoever it was he knew very well and that was the holy cow in the next van who complained about his music and about his van rocking when he got lucky. In the mornings when they all carried their slop pails down to the toilet and washing area she used a Grecian urn, carrying it in both hands with a pink towel over the top, as though she did something different. Inside the van was shock.

'Shit!'

Somebody had been in. Somebody had got a screwdriver and taken his bed to pieces. Why had Kathleen not allowed friendly PC Sid to get his noddy pal in and catch them red-handed? Because she knew something that Marchmont could now guess. That Finbow's sex aids in their most obscene and illegal manifestations were stashed in his locked wardrobe, secure from police raids on the shop. Hard porn, probably. He checked the wardrobe and it was still locked. Holy Cow was paranoid about his bed. It was now mid-morning and he left his van and went over to hers; it had been made to look like an ivy-covered thatched cottage. The door was locked but he forced it, putting his shoulder against it. She screamed as he came in, she was in bed with a man and getting rocked.

'Horace!' she said. It took a moment to attract the chap's attention because he was nearly there. Holy Cow sat up and held a pink sheet around her breast, staring at Marchmont. 'How dare you! Get out! Get out! Oh, my God, please help me!' Marchmont felt quite foolish but had to be fierce for a little longer. 'What have you done to my fucking bed? You religious maniac!'

'Are you Mr Marchmont?' her lover said. He was not young, but artistic and bearded and with interesting poached eggs under his eyes. It was Horace Spurgeon Fenton, the writer. Claude was ten years old and visiting his dad last time they met. Laboriously the man climbed over the woman and reached for his truss, trying to get himself together without being detected. He was talking but his voice was too deep to be understood by humans and Marchmont said, 'Are you saying something to me?' Horace nodded, wiped his nose on his finger, very embarrassed. 'I took your bed to pieces – I'm sorry. I'm going to put it together again now. I just came around really to borrow a screwdriver from Flossie – this is Flossie. But I expect you know that. We were neighbours – you're living in my van. You're not a bit like Albert. Everybody's been saying you're like Albert.'

But Marchmont was not talking any more until he knew what was what. He apologised to the lady and left. Later she made him some rock cakes and he told her about his father's Jehovah's Witnesses, leavening it as exemplary of God in life. But that was not now. Now was Horace the writer tapping at the door with a softness in his eye, like a returning dog. He had lived here in the harsh winter following the heatwave summer of '59. With him was Diane, a girl crippled by a rock that fell on her in Rutland after a mad drive from Augustus John's Studio Club in Swallow Street.

'My hernia gave way at the wrong moment,' Horace explained to Marchmont, who was watching him restore his fitted bed. There were diamonds in the wall, now on the draining board after being washed. These, Horace had come to collect. 'You're lucky they're here. They were going to pulp these vans. There's a new road coming through.' Then Marchmont, alive with new perceptions, said: 'You keep in touch, don't you. Who is it – Kathleen?' Horace smiled round at him. He and Diane had smashed two beds, he told the lad.

'I smuggled these stones from Rome as part of a film scripting deal. Di Sica! To tell you the truth,

66

Marchy, I was terrified of them. Happy to leave them here – when I got back Arturo was dead. I won't go into it.'

Marchmont knew the feeling. One of the diamonds rolled down the sink and vanished and neither of them mentioned it, that casual was the feeling. The entrapped tally boy watched the entrapped novelist sort out more than a score of diamonds and divide them into two parts, dropping one lot in his own pocket and giving Claude Marchmont the rest – 'Please! I insist. You've been sitting on a bomb – these belong partly to Fortunato's the caterers, partly to Arturo's widow and partly to the Mussolini family, all original luminants of World Films. You know Arturo was ripped off while he was in prison – the alien thing. We'll take them on his behalf, boy – he suffered. He was in the ship of aliens that got torpedoed – he jumped holding his life jacket to his chest. The others let them flap and got their necks broken when they hit the water. Arturo's best friend had his head blown off, just the top, he was calling to Arturo to join him on the rescue net and Arturo could see his brains! So please – enjoy! For me this is for Albert – I am looking after Tres and the baby in Jersey – ' Marchmont stopped him with a surrendering and yielding pocketing of the diamonds. They were worth – some of them, the rare pink gems – when laundered at least a cool million. Who needs train robberies?

'Do you want to take me to the airport?'

'Why not?' said Marchmont.

Flossie at her door watering the geraniums waved them away. 'Is the jazz band still on the site?' asked

Horace. There was Rod on trumpet and Tony on bass and always a prowl car with its bum hidden in some dark gateway. At the boarding gate at Heathrow the writer put something in the lad's hand, hidden. 'I owe your father this, tell him *No Hiding Place* and *Market In Honey Lane* and see if he remembers!' It was a french letter.

Leaving Terminal 1 Marchmont saw the shaven headed man that Kathleen had shot, now watching him from a pile of luggage, standing as if waiting or minding it. When the man caught Marchmont's eye he came across and said excuse me – he was wearing a bright alpaca American suit and Hawaiian shirt and tight straw hat for the beach, though the baldness was accentuated around the ears.

'Hah?' said Marchmont.

'Hey, is this the place you go to the Channel Islands from? I don't think it is. My friend went in and vanished – I think he's gone some place else. I mean, we met in Soho last night in this club – do you smoke these, sir?'

'Are you putting me on?' Marchy asked.

The man expressed pained surprise. 'No sir. I think this guy has been putting me on.' He looked around at the oddly directioned non-direction people and the officials and police and drivers and became nervous. 'These places bug me – I think this goes to inter-continental, y'know? Have you just seen somebody off yourself? Did he go to Jersey, did you notice? My friend has gone to Jersey – but this is his luggage, dammit. I've been here an hour.' It occurred to Marchmont now that this was not the murdered man. He offered to look after the luggage while the

American searched for his missing link. An hour later Marchmont walked away. It was a joke. What they call a link joke. Like holding one end of a ladder. The tally boy drove fast for his appointment with fear. And if that was not the Jersey terminal, where was Horace going? Or was it Horace? Are these diamonds genuine? I hope not, he thought. The car remained beautiful. He polished it every time he got out of it. Some things are real. It has to be said here that Marchmont saw the shaven-headed man six or seven times more in his lifetime, sometimes walking, sometimes serving in street markets or driving a bus. On the bad days he wore a wig.

6

A little tiny weeny small kind of spider swung down like a trapeze artist to greet a medium longish fly from the woods, a slightly green one which had been trying to get unstuck. That was Marchmont, Marchmont thought, lying in his caravan bed. Not quite comfortably. People put things back slightly crooked in some way. For twenty years you walk with a limp. This Marchmont did anyway and one of the things that made him feel closer to Kathleen, the Irish rose, than he really wished to feel, was that she had detected this personal handicap and in her ceaselessly busy republican mind had connected it at some conversational point with a gap in his past.

'Frankie Vaughan started singing in a speakeasy in The Gut, that's in Valetta in Malta, during his national service and Peter Sellars played the drums and Spike Milligan played bits of gas piping – though that was Hitler's War – and so on, yet you never mention your national service and you must be about the same age – and I know you're not a conchie, although we all are in principle – are you awake?'

This was Kathleen waking up first on the undelivered mattress and getting bored.

'I was in the coal mines, I was a Bevan boy. I didn't have flat feet.' And then she told him what he had, which only lovers know. His long nose and his comic eyebrows and his bouncing negro gait and his constant give me five, five, five, man, was to complement and conceal a limp following polio at age eleven when it hit the forty-seven, -eight and -nine postwar babies with the issue of deaf aids and other punishments for killing each other.

'That is correct,' said Marchmont, as Albert used to say. Never be long-winded, in other words. The silkworm producing Finbow undies comes from Vladivostok, madam. The spider now did a brilliant thing, squatting in front of the fly and spinning it round at a dizzy speed until it was a parcel. The little tiny weeny small kind of spider now trudged away up the corner of the dew-laden aluminium window frame of the Berkeley caravan tugging its dinner behind it. Now a sparrow appeared like a puppet, upside down from the rain gutter above the window, and ate spider and fly in one perky snap of its beak, looked in at Marchmont, then vanished into the Hermitage Park woodland.

'That's me,' Marchy thought gloomily. He did not mean that he was the sparrow.

The whole gang was in tonight, righty? Marchmont was to be killed, rubbed out. Only he knew that it was not his fault, because Kathleen had gone to Bedford for a pacifist meeting. She needs it, was Marchy's thought when Brown dog barked the news

71

at the shop when he called in for her to save two lots of petrol and keeping, more importantly, one sober to drive back in the early hours.

'Come in, Marchmont, I want to talk to you – ' This was Oliver Hardy, but not twiddling his tie, Gerry Chapman the Gestapo and MI6 special double-agent. 'And I want to talk to you, baby,' said Colonel Reiner Wertzen of the top secret US Russia-watching base at Chicksands. Although our hero had not got the details he did realise that he was going to die. The Irish question was there, the funding of the IRA, the mounting of criminal projects for the boys. Ruby at the Liverpool end of the train robbery. The club had quietened at Marchmont's entrance. He made a desperate Albert entrance gag, one of three:

'Carry on as if I was just an ordinary person!'

Kathleen might have got the ball in the air from there but nobody here wanted to save his life. Villain faces peered round from billiard tables and three girls wore the illegal frocks. The lovely Indian girl had been singing in a sari but now stood quietly until his throat was cut, drawing up her sari to cover all but her lovely eyes. Alfie Bass, Victor Maddern, Leo McKern, Ronald Lacy and Leslie Dwyer broke back from the bar and a bottle smashed somewhere. These were the actor names current in the crime movies and television series that Kathleen and Marchy used to name. That's Harry Towb – the girls were all Shirley Ann Fields or from Cliveden. Sometimes brought in from Boreham Wood, their mothers studio cleaners and tea-makers, their fathers commissionaires.

'So you had to follow me back to base, hah?' This

was Helga's father, Marchmont felt certain. He was going to be executed for the crimes of Albert Argyle. 'Who are you working for?' asked Chapman. Marchmont wanted to appeal to his decency, by claiming a double agency – as he genuinely had with Hoover and Hot Point on the tally round. 'Could I have a drink?' Marchy asked.

Gerry said, as if he had heard the request before, 'Give him a drink and a cigarette.'

'I didn't follow you back, Colonel – I drove straight up to Clophill to see my girl – ' he saw Chapman stiffen and corrected it ' – this girl, she's just a friend.' Chapman said: 'Don't two-time Kathleen, she wants to marry you when this is over.' He meant, not when the train robbery is successfully carried out, but when she has stopped fucking me on my boat. When I don't need her any more she will marry you. She is catholic Irish and she will not be unfaithful within the holy vows. Marchmont might have taken offence under any other circumstances.

'Reiner, he wasn't following us.' This was the Sam Kidd driver who must have been in the support car with the rear-viewing video. 'I told you he wasn't, sir. He was up our arse twice – that's not professional.' The colonel was reluctant to let go of his ruthless image – he was Rod Steiger. 'I didn't say he was professional, nobody's saying Marchmont is professional – '

'Oh, come on, Reiner,' said Gerry, 'Marchmont was in prison for stabbing his girl friend.' This impressed everybody and little Alfie Bass, as if asking for further reference, said: 'Did she die?' Marchmont could not claim that it was just an invention of his to get the job with Kathleen. By thought association Gerry said: 'Tell the colonel about your mother, Marchy – she's in a lunatic asylum.'

'I didn't realise,' the colonel said.

'She writes cowboy novels,' Marchmont told him. 'She writes under different names. Her readers call her Tex and Clyde and Calico Slim.'

'Well I'm sorry, Marchmont. We all have women like that in the family – some of them with horses. It was just that you don't seem to be that rich or have form, y'know – what's that? You dropped something?' Another Albert inspiration, as if from the lonely graves of last year, helping the lad along – he had dropped a diamond.

'It looks like this,' he said, holding another one up in his fingers. 'If you can't find it, it doesn't matter – leave it for the singer.' She dropped her face mask and would do more, everybody groping around and flashing lighters.

'He's in rocks, then?' Reiner Wertzen had taken Gerry Chapman back to the bar. 'You should tell me these things, Gerry – I had a stiffs truck laid on.' There was an unspoken professional subscription to nothing harming Claude Marchmont until they knew where he kept the rest. The strategy for the forthcoming train robbery was laid down in a non-secretive fashion, it being understood you got nailed to the floor with this particular coterie. The biggest millions of old bank notes got taken by the Travelling Post Office on certain days and nights of the year and zero was August plus Ruby's final pigeon.

'You piss off abroad for four weeks, everybody on the list. What you do afterwards is nothing, and the

74

fuzz know that – right, Gordon?' Gordon was a superintendent at Watford. 'But what you do before the job, that is the give-away! Right, Henry?' Old Henry was there. It was said afterwards that five policemen got pubs. The publican that said it gassed himself with his dogs a few weeks later. 'We are going abroad,' Gerry told them. 'I do not want to know where. No fucking wish you were here! We have no connection.'

'What about this place?' asked Marchmont, unthinkingly.

Mistake. They all looked at him. Alfie Bass or his look-alike, repeated his previous interest. 'Did she die? Your girlfriend?'

'Jill is in an asylum with my mother,' Marchy said.

'That's nice,' said the Indian singer. She and Marchmont had already, since the diamond dropping, exchanged contractual glances. Gerry said, 'I am turning this place over to Elizabeth as a health farm – ' Marchmont nodded in his trendy way, people really need homeopathic treatment and educated diets, you get murder, you get robbery, you get corruption plus a social message. The boy began to feel at home now. He would tread carefully with Gerry's caretaker attitude about Kathleen and he must find out more about Niloufar, which meant cherry blossom and what the American connection might be. It was explained quite quickly and believably when Kathleen and Elizabeth came into South Mymms Lodge – the name of Gerry's in the Country – from their anti-nuking, or whatever it was tore their dresses and made them laughably muddy.

Colonel Wertzen opened champagne and Chelsea

Ted came in as if connected to the cork, a girl in his hands. 'What have *you* been doing in the fields?' Elizabeth Chapman asked the Leo McKern figure, who had just asked them the same thing. 'They're bringing the new high-pressure gas across country from the North Sea,' the American told Marchmont. 'We get it first on the yank bases and then our friends here, Gerry and the Pacemakers – the dollar does it. England waits.'

Marchmont felt relieved. It was not that criminal. Only the money seemed criminal, the men digging the long pipe lines stayed in the Hilton and bought cottages at Ashburnham and Tring – the gas labourers. They got, those staying at the Tollaini Brothers' Thatched Barn, as much a week as Dennis Price was getting down the road for playing Jeeves.

'How do you dig trenches?' Marchmont found himself asking, idiotically, over the last, very last, departure drinks, Kathleen laughing at him. It is entirely an Irish thing. It is an Irish thing entirely. On the long road home he gave her the love of Horace Spurgeon Fenton, the characterful old writer, recounting his plans for Tres and Albert's baby and by association wondering about his disenchanted widow, Alice Finbow as was and her autistic child.

'Are you going to screw that Indian girl, then?'

'And get hepatitis, the serious kind – B?' Then he said, as Bignell's Corner came up, 'That's only a joke – I love Indians. They are like children or they are like professors or they are clothcap English with a king and queen – which we don't even think about.'

At Bignell's corner where Barnet By-pass crosses St Albans to Barnet A6, Kathleen hit a car that was out of petrol and being pushed across against the lights. A man lay shouting for help in the upside-down car until he died, Marchmont holding his hand. The dead man's wife, Christine, had a fractured skull, Kathleen was face-smashed by the windscreen, three children with lesser injuries, brought together in a hurry of trolleys and young expressionless medics and silent screaming noise at the Redhill Hospital at Edgware on the A5, south and beyond the beginning of their ride home together in the shiny white bull-nosed Rover. Farther than anywhere they ever went from Hitchin. On a level, he thought, waiting for the news, laterally, of the cricket in the recreation ground at Little Berkhamstead, the first mini-skirt and the ice-cream. You need not have driven as far south as that coming from Billericay to Hitchin. Buntingford, Baldock, Letchworth, Hitchin, he might have come and got home quicker. He could have been with her a lot of times. Quicker.

7

Says:

'Are you the surgeon? Is she all right? Is she alive?'

'I dunno, mate – I'm a cleaner.'

'Oh, shit – hi! Hi! Excuse me – my wife's in there.'

'Oh, she'll be all right, Mr Finbow. She's anaes-thetised at the moment. I've been taking out the bits and pieces – her bones have chipped, brow, cheek and nose. Mercifully the glass doesn't splinter – her face went through it.'

'I tried to hold her, I could see it coming. That family pushing that car right across the road, the chap behind the wheel, two kids and mum pushing, you often see them, in the rain going down long roads out of petrol. He's got a big car and no money to run it – he won't need money now. What about Kathleen's teeth and that?'

'They're okay – they were on the floor, luckily. I expect that was the impact. She could have got whiplash. I'm Tim Hapgood if you want me.'

'When can I see her?'

'Not yet – she's been asking for you, over and

over, Eric, Eric, Eric, amazing under deep sedation. Are you Eric?'

'No. Didn't she say Albert?'

'No, I'm sorry old chap – I didn't realise. But they'll say anything under Penthadine, fantasies. Are you Albert?'

'No. Not yet . . .'

The young surgeon pressed Marchmont's arm and grinned at him. 'I know what you're saying!'

'This boy was only fifteen and split between two homes, his mum and sister and his dad with a girlfriend.' Gamble's crew nodded her head, experienced in all domestic permutations. 'I tell you what got me,' Charlie said. 'He left a will.'

'Left a what?'

'The boy drew up a last will and testament – all his toys and where to take them, books, aeroplane, skates – oh Christ!' The boy had then walked up the railway embankment and lay across a line holding his ears. He had had his tea. 'Please don't go on, Charlie. We've got to see Hammond in a minute.' Hammond's wife Midge was the late customer of Marchmont's that he would never mention. She had been given to him by Hetty at Callendar's after Albert was killed in the bushes. Hetty was then another trading stamp customer and Luton had shifted its decade of musical chairs.

The house appeared to be shut up.

'I came here last week and the kids were all here,' Vicky said. 'I helped him wash up. I hope I didn't say anything to upset him.' The two police officers, uniformed, fretted at the locked front door of the council house. 'He hasn't got a gun,' Inspector Gamble said. He leaned over the hedge and banged on the neighbour's door.

A woman popped up from behind her hedge across the road, holding a tiny cupressus macracarpa in her hand, her best tablespoon full of mud in the other. 'Can I help you?' They asked about the widower and his motherless kids and his time-table and habits and Wednesday. It was Wednesday, the second Wednesday in July with August ahead. President Kennedy safely in Seattle, at Boeings. Trains hurrying from Liverpool to Euston, London. Gerry Chapman and his coterie all over the Med and further, strangers every one, in new little sunny circles, establishing fresh identities, making new friends. Some were so happy they would not come back for the big job.

'They haven't gone out,' the woman shouted. 'I've been out here in the garden all the morning.' She vanished. Vicky said, 'I'll break in at the back – I can smell gas. I don't know though. I could smell it last time.' Charlie Gamble smelt it all the time now. Not the new gas.

They had smashed the back door with a garden roller and run all over the house when Mr Hammond came in the front door with a straggle of kids eating sweets and ice cream, him carrying a loaded plastic carrier and a long loaf under the other arm. He looked up the stairs from the front hall, Vicky and Charlie craned round from the bannisters. 'What you doing up there?'

'I'm sorry, sir – I take full responsibility. We couldn't make you hear.' He was in Fine Fare, he explained, everything covered in politeness. The neighbour said they hadn't gone out. 'No, well, I wait for them to go in or go away – they mean well, but I can't get past them without, you know – I've asked for a transfer, change houses. Like a cup of tea?'

'Our uniforms don't help, do they?' Vicky said.

'Thass all right.'

'Mum! Mum! I want some lemonade!'

Wait a minute, getting called mum now without even noticing it; the police wanted to scram. The police were leagues behind Marchmont, still inquiring about Finbow's missing furniture and if Midge Hammond was in debt. She wasn't in debt. She was having an affair with somebody. The kids had dispersed and they had three tea bags in the kitchen. 'Police's allus here one time.' His shire speech had come back after the enforced etiquettes of love. 'Why was that then?' asked Charlie, at home with him now, also Herts and Beds.

'About gun licenses and that, tightening up. We used to take a pot, everybody – rabbits and that.'

'Mixy's coming back,' said the girl.

The gun was lost and the talk was Midge's state of mind for the overdose. 'I killed her,' he said, suddenly, as if he had just thought of it or just remembered. The inspector forked his foot to shut the children out of it. They didn't say anything but waited for Hammond to control his throat. He was Nicholas, aged thirty-eight and known as Nikky on the building sites and at the Crown.

It was not going to be a hanging matter, Charlie Gamble could see from Vicky's compassion, which she now conveyed to him, explaining the murder. 'She bumped his car. Dented it. He went off at her – it wasn't that!'

'I shouted at her. I shouted at her. Where she been late and that with the car, on and on, wouldn't let it rest – she was working all hours! She paid for the fucking thing – sorry! Sorry! She did cleaning and that. I wasn't her lover. My breath smelt. Beer and onions and only clean them in the mornings, sometimes not that. What's that toilet roll on the bed? she say. What's that doing? She kept a lovely bedroom, green glass dressing-table stuff from Callendar's or Finbow's or Lawsons or pink stamps and that, little luxuries, dainty she was, Midge. I spit in that, I told her – in the night, bit of paper, catarrh and that, in the family. My mum always had little screws of paper by the bed. Rings of white where she stood her glass of stomach stuff. She didn't have anybody to worry about after dad went. Got killed at Arras. But I had Midge and I killed her – there was somebody else and I don't blame her. Beer belly and that, never get it up or anything. Take her pissed sometimes. I passed water one night in the wardrobe, on her things. She couldn't put up with that and she couldn't leave the kids and then I shouted at her.'

'Mum!' came the child's cry.

'I'm going to get the dinner for them,' the WPC said, 'You two have a chat.' 'Tell Lucy,' said dad, 'She's a good 'un.' Gamble lit him a ciggy.

'Will you marry again?' Inspector Gamble asked Hammond. 'I dunno. I'll have to smarten myself up. I might go to night school. Midge wanted me to go with her to marriage guidance. Then she did German

82

instead. I spend too much time at the Crown. She hates pubs. She's got a friend who wants to abolish pubs – some chap she met. Instead of pubs you have drinking bars, family bars, like Barcelona and Benidorm. Wine and coffee. You don't have to pay for it.' Charlie queried that but Nick Hammond was vague about his wife's radical chums. 'There was a chap come round selling at Luton who wanted to turn the Thames red – the whole river. Midge liked things like that.'

'I should think that was Albert – did he work for Callendar's? That was Albert – he got shot.'

'That's right! That's when the police come asking about my gun licence – were you at Luton, then, Mr Gamble?' Gamble wasn't but Sid was and Sid rang bells, PC Nation was full of Albert anecdotes. Inspector Gamble was about to put his foot in it and although Victoria came in to hear it, she could not stop it. 'I don't know why they come to me,' the husband said. 'It wasn't just you, Nick!' The WPC knew that her superior officer would now follow that remark with a man-to-man laugh. She tried to think of something to change the subject but the subject was silence.

'Oh, I see,' said Mr Hammond. Tally boys had never occurred to him. 'The potatoes are on, Mr Hammond,' Vicky told him. He met her eyes for a moment.

'That was a rotten blunder,' she said, back in the car and moving. Charlie covered his face in shame and the radio spoke, telling them of Kathleen Finbow's car crash yesterday. 'That's outside our area, Barnet By-pass – anybody hurt?'

'One dead – her boyfriend I expect, he was behind the wheel.' They'd got the wrong car.

'That's Mr Marchmont,' said the crew. After the tally boy conversation it sounded like God at work. 'Proud'll be down there,' Gamble predicted. He was wondering how it was the Hammonds had had first Albert and then Marchmont in their married lives, in two different towns at two different times. 'They were living with his mother, then,' the WPC told him, efficiently. They still couldn't find out where the fraud was. Vicky and Charlie were the Hitchin sector of the East Herts Police fraud squad.

'I'll try the vicar again,' said the inspector.

'I liked Mr Marchmont,' she said. She had his Teasmade. 'As she said it, not a word of a lie,' Gamble told his wife Gemma, 'Marchy's big white Rover Hundred whizzed past us going the other way – not a scratch on it! He was alive!' Amazing, his wife said, getting on with her *My Weekly*. But that was Wednesday night, meanwhile he braked the motor and reversed and followed Marchmont back to the caravan park.

'Don't go in,' the girl said, crisply. When people were not dead, that was fraud. And honey I miss you was in her head, coming home in the middle of the day and finding her crying over the dented car.

They got Claude Marchmont with a car load of sex aids and diamonds in the lining of his belted sports jacket, light brown corduroy.

'You can't arrest me, can you?' They hadn't arrested him, they had just taken his shoes off. The arrival of Superintendent Nathan Proud was awaited.

He was at some unspecified place near Kathleen Finbow. Marchy and Charlie and Victoria looked at their watches, estimating the distance back. He would have taken a tasteful (cheap) bunch of freesias. Marchmont knew what to look for in Kathleen's bed: freesias or else a spider with Tipp-ex on its leg. That was Gerry.

'Sorry to keep you waiting, Mr Marchmont!'

'I think he's asleep, sir,' the WPC explained.

'He's a hero,' said the super. 'He climbed in, everywhere covered in petrol, and held this chap's hand until he died.'

'Put his shoes on, Vicky,' Gamble said.

Not surprisingly, there was absolutely nothing fraudulent about him. The little black parcels and the plain labelled devices and the magazines and descriptive literature and photographs were confiscated for further investigation. The diamonds were his own and Marchy was off the hook. His car, the best and strongest and most handsome thing Rover ever did, was almost unscratched. In love with Kathleen now, what with her teeth and a mummy-bandaged face he had rushed back home to empty the locked wardrobe, destroy the whole dirty business and go to Butlins.

8

'Nobody knew he was unhappy. He was good at school. Imagine how his mum and dad feel, grumbling or shouting or telling him off, like any other family, that's all. They both loved him of course they did, specially as they were separated, I mean I was in a broken home, used to stay with dad sometimes – it's not a suicidal thing at all, there's more variety for the kids, they don't know about humping especially in Dublin – '

'You don't half look funny talking under those bandages, mate – does it hurt?'

'Then he had his tea and after tea he wrote his will – his mum thought he was doing his homework.'

'Don't cry. You're crying. It's coming through. How did you read about it?'

'I didn't – the sister read it to me, I couldn't sleep with you gone.'

'That's nice.'

Sister came over from her desk and clapped her hands, like a decided child. 'We're going to take some of that laundry off your face, Mrs Finbow – put some glue on it instead, much nicer, pink, smells like acid drops.' They wanted Marchmont out of the way for the screens to go up and he went for a walk. Gave his car a polish. Christine Viger was all right, no fracture, just concussion. The children were already home with their nana. And their dad was all right with his bird, somewhere, or married again. The man that died, Christine's boyfriend, did not seem very important. Never any money.

Although she was a mystery in many forbidden areas of her life, mostly connected to Gerry and to her dubious businesses, Kathleen had somehow connected immediately to Marchmont, as with an instant umbilical cord. Which was the stabbing of his girlfriend, as related by Eric. Now with Eric Finbow gone, the relationship had cemented; like were like, mother and son and lovers. The uglier she got, the more his security. She was not ugly but he knew what he meant. She was trying hard.

'Tell me what you think . . .'

'Oh Jesus!'

'Oh come on, Marchmont! It's not that bad!'

It was not that bad. But seeing the best he had seen the worst, seen her with a broken neck. He was nearly on his own in the world. Dad at Billericay, mother in a nut house, George in his leavable marriage. He thanked God for the Rover. Kathleen nursed Marchy's head to her breast for a moment, the screen still surrounding them. 'Tell me about the sausages . . .' Outside in the ward the sisters smiled at the laughter.

'Would it disappoint you to know that I have never been to prison and I never stabbed my girlfriend?'

'No, it wouldn't. It brings you closer to me, somehow. It's much more colourful and imaginative to invent things.'

'And I didn't invent it.'

'Then I hate you! Say!'

That was an Albert line, which they both knew. Marchmont told her. Somebody at Rumbolds had told him what he had heard about him. Wrongly, but Marchmont could see its value immediately. This was a six foot new town planner with a Porsche, coughing nervously and keeping his distance. Marchy had stuck his 'for sale' pole in the ground and said haugh! in peace. 'I won't tell Gerry it's not true, he thinks a lot of you – so does Henry.' Marchy remembered Henry from the briefing. He was a high up policeman. 'Henry Wannamaker,' she told him. 'He fixed the world series – that's what we call it now since Gatsby. Wannamaker fixed the four million old fiver pulping heist from Reed's paper mill in Rochester – remember one bale dropped off the crane and broke open? The security was all up at ground level and the gang went in with the pulp barge under the river mill.'

'What's Wannamaker doing in the train robbery?'

'Never say train robbery.'

There was only three weeks to go and because of the accident, Kathleen and Marchmont were the only people on the list not yet dispersed. And they could not contact anybody because it was forbidden and nobody knew where anybody was. Marchmont, who knew less than anybody about the big job, had assumed Kathleen and Gerry were flying off to Rio together for a big pre-fixture hump, but not so. She filled him in once more as the nurses took away the bed screens and visitors came in with grapes.

'If somebody knows where somebody is it will compromise somebody and create lies under interrogation and getting beaten in your cells and so on – for instance if you knew where Niloufer the Cherry Blossom was? Also you would be nailed to the floor by the list.' Marchmont realised that she was being jealous. Trying to tell him something. She gave it time to sink in, then asked him if he got his diamond back. Which he had not.

'Do you watch James Bond?' She had decided to keep him there all night. She told him about the dispersal strategy as it applied itself in movies, Elstree, down the road from the club. There were seven James Bonds in *Casino Royale* and the producers, Saltzman and Broccoli, sent the seven actors all over the world to lose themselves for a year before production. Their faces had to be forgotten by the public, no commericals or chat shows, low profile, disappear, going, going, gone. 'John Gregson vanished!' Marchy remembered.

'No – he was badly cast. Jimmy went – Monica's boyfriend.' Marchmont didn't quite see the parallel and also a little black girl with pigtails was sitting on Kathleen's bed swinging her legs and listening. Because hospitals become boring unless the loved one is dying. Marchy got fidgety and Kathleen released his hand. 'Where will you go from here? Like tonight? All by yourself in Hitchin?'

'Stevenage,' Marchmont told her and she became

quietly angry. Her scars under the bits of glue turned red and her nostrils quivered, though she could not let go with the little girl now engrossed. 'I knew you'd say that – indoor bowls on a hot August bank holiday. Everybody's gone pale since the Indians took it over – Niloufer on the cash desk in a mini sari and no bra.'

'Is she?' Marchmont did not know that. 'But she's on the list. She'll be back in the Taj Mahal now. That's farther than Clacton.' He did something with his eyebrows and made her laugh and then she asked a nurse if she could smoke and she could, since she had cleared the anaesthetic out of her lungs and then she felt in Marchmont's fine belted corduroy sports jacket pocket for ciggies and came out with the french letter. Child or no child she pulled a china bedpan out of her cupboard and hit him with it, contents and all. Marchmont fell unconscious between the ward beds and melèe ensued. He was taken away for X-ray and the bell went early to get rid of everybody.

'Do you want tea, Mrs Finbow?'

Everything quickly back to order except Kathleen, now crying over dead lovers, but quickly sorted out. Marchmont had kept his eyes closed until safely out of her reach. Soon was back with her bringing a box of Roses chocolates and a bottle of Lucozade, his forehead plastered. They kissed and he told her about Horace and the No Hiding Place and Malcolm in Billericay.

'You should have told me. I remember that! They picked up two girls outside Rediffusion in Kingsway and took them back to those big blocks of flats near Lords – your father hadn't got a french letter and

Horace always had two – so they say – me and Eric were in the same house at Hampstead, both dancing.'

'It sounds like it.'

'Sylvia, my best friend, she's an exotic dancer, remember the Frazer Hayes Quartet and Dill Jones and Dudley Moore's trio – well, Eric played banjo and rode a trick bicycle – '

'Excuse me,' he rested the gabbling alibi lady back on her pillow. 'I don't need all that. This is only a scratch. I tell you what – keep the froggie till you come out.' They parted in good humour.

That night, ever so late, Niloufer came to the caravan in the middle of *Eleanor Rigby* and the Beatles and she stayed all night, paying for the diamond. She had got a round thousand pounds for hers and she had a buyer for Marchmont's little pile of nine cut rocks, now in a properly tie-necked piece of soft leather. She told him that her father was the health minister in Ceylon, which put him at ease. Having made no positive move himself to be unfaithful, he did not feel guilty. In the morning he drove down to Bute Street and took over the shop, bright as a pin. He realised that he had enough money for a partnership, a good car and did not need the train robbery. He did not know and neither did she, that the Indian girl was pregnant.

Marchmont knew something more important than fatherhood. The silly farcical situation that had come about between them in the hospital, had given him what Christ had seen when he wept. Albert was not all bad. Albert was Marchmont's true genesis, this he

91

now saw. And he felt clearly his pre-natal relationship with Kathleen Ryan and her relationship with his own father, Malcolm. She was gabbling on because the bottom of the well was too naked to be anything but the truth. All of this came out in Marchmont's fresh interest in dildos.

'Rosie – come here. Explain some of these medical bits and pieces to me. I'm going to display them in the window – our sex aids will have a window. I may start the first sex shop – that's what Mr Finbow was going to do when he got drowned.' Browning watched Marchmont all the morning, delving into the secrets with Rosie and Gloria and Jen – who happened to come in; more and more after that. She lived in Wilstead and drove ten miles.

'There's nothing dirty about it, that's the point,' he told the vicar. 'I'm going to call it The Sausage Factory.' It did seem to leaven it, add humour. They would run a save-a-marriage week. On the Friday, the week following the accident and with Kathleen due out tomorrow, Ruby came into the shop.

'It's all set to go,' she told Marchy.

'Oh? What's that, then?'

'I like your gear,' she said. 'Are you coming home?'

At seven, stopping at the Three Moorhens for a quickie, he drove Ruby back to the brothel, the first two birds on the list to home in. 'How do you like my new hair?' she asked him, in bed that night.

'Is it really yours?' It was like a soft pile carpet and had embarrassed him on the other position, being boylike. She had grown it during her various male and female wig projects, mostly during the day with the travelling post office despatch. She had been placed by the International Red Cross in Cadogan Square, a note of secondment from a Lady Lewis saying that she was writing up a vital job article for the *Guardian*.

'How does Gerry Chapman organise that?'

'I'll tell you something,' Ruby said. 'Don't find out – you'll live longer.'

In the rest of the bordello Mary and Di were holding a nudie party, partly barbecued into the woods of Bush End. These parties among the hookers and their many clients and relations and friends – they had a choir, civil rights demos – were always promotional of Kathleen's stock.

'How is Kathleen?' Ruby said.

'We're going to get married at Halloween,' Marchmont decided, suddenly, nodding his long nose into her various breasts.

Lady came in to the embers of the bonfire party, couples under blankets and men tipping bottles, stirred the fire with the toe of her riding boot. 'Hey – what you got here? A hoedown? Name's Ross Woods. Looking for my boy Claude. Claude Marchmont?'

She had on a white shirt with a check riding skirt and a yellow duster scarf tied on her shoulder, a low-crowned dirty cream and crushed cowboy hat. She was made up like Joan Crawford in *Destry Rides Again* with painted face and lips and double eyelashes, thick with mascara and with scalped settlers' skulls for ear rings. 'God, I wish I'd thought of that!' said Mary Mowlem to her friend Di, now in the blanket. They told her where Marchy was and then some of them went across to look at her motor bike, a big AJS, circa 1929. 'I've read her books,' Mary said. '*Harness The Wind*, *Texas Tapestry*, *Calico City* – that's where the hero gets hijacked after his trail south with the cattle? Kathleen's got them all. Ross was brought up in Bricket Wood on Zane Grey and she's never been farther west than High Wycombe – J. T. Edson was a postman and John Harvey plays the violin. Do you read westerns, Tom?' Her boyfriend was Chief Inspector Tom Saunders, still fighting the folk museum war and getting not quite nowhere; he got further without his son. There came the sound of a six-gun from the house and Marchmont's scream – silly scream.

'What's the drink doing?' asked Di. They trailed back to their rooms, leaving the lonely fire and the hay bales for sitting, stolen from the fields. 'This is Ruby,' Marchmont was saying. 'Ruby, this is mum.' Glad to know yuh. There was no great reunion. Ross had heard that Claude had money and Horace had money and there was a flat in Wimbledon – she could come out of the asylum again.

'What's your father doing in Billericay?'

'He can't move till he gets another girl with a job.'

'You give him some diamonds, dammit – no, let Horace give him diamonds. Horace owes him diamonds. Buy Lorel some beads, Guinness and cigarettes – some more teeth. She keeps throwing them away, losing them.' Ruby knew about the autistic one, the mother moving in with her sometimes, the optimum option. 'She's not daft,' Ross would say. 'There'd be nothing wrong with Lorel in a cow town.' George was a worry. He was too solid and had a job.

Marchmont fixed his mother coffee and beans and told her about his getting married to Kathleen and the accident and nothing about anything else. Being a mother, she knew about everything else. 'Bill Howard saw you at Gerry's club,' she remarked. Bill was her publisher, film man, editor, a good solid part of the Marchmont family life ever since he had met Horace Spurgeon Fenton in Trafalgar Square in the rain in 1951. Albert was the catalyst, Albert and Horace and Malcolm and Ross and Gerry and Kathleen and Di and Mary and Lorel and Fleet Street and Elstree is the name of the book. There were lateral connections into watching families or equivalent tribes and sometimes somebody died. 'Don't go to prison,' Ross told the lad.

Word came at five in the morning that Gerry Chapman was dying in Brazil. Kathleen on the hospital phone, sitting in the staff office. 'You have got to fly out and save his life. I had a call from International Red Cross in New York giving me a telephone number in Rio and the doctor's name which is Spanish though he speaks English – have you got a pen ready? Marchmont? Marchmont?'

'Put his head back,' Ross was telling Ruby, Marchmont now fainted back onto his chair. 'Hold on a second, Kathleen,' the cowgirl said to the phone. It was a nose bleed, Claude's other reaction to something bigger than himself. Nose bleed news it was; with the biggest crime of the century just about to pull out from Liverpool South, the keeper of the matrix had got himself bitten by a mosquito. The immune system, as in all life on this planet, controlled life and death. There was only one elixir in science to save the great smuggler, double-agent and fat man and that was available only in England – in a backward country, backward becomes a virtue. Marchmont at last caught up with Kathleen, his mother helping to support the telephone receiver in his pale hands.

'This is brandy, darling,' Ruby told him, quietly. He nodded, his sooted eyes rolling like a gollywog on a jar of marmalade. Master-mind Marchmont. 'Spell it,' he said. As Kathleen spelt it, Marchy spoke it and Ruby wrote it down. The life-saving word was Q-U-I-N-I-N-E. 'That's quinine,' said Joan Crawford, 'everybody knows quinine, I used to give you kids quinine for a fever.' She repeated this to the telephone. It was quinine but Gerry had malaria caught in the Matto Grosso from a second generation mosquito – its poison was immune to quinine and immune to all known antibiotics and his only chance was to get his chest surgically opened and have liquid quinine pumped directly into his ventricles – his heart. In all the world, including New York, quinine now came only in tablets.

'What is your Malcolm like to live with?' Ruby asked Ross in the course of all this telephoning. There was New York, there was Lady Lewis in Cadogan Square and a Doctor David Murray in the House of Lords, an expert epidemicist with a detailed route to Brasilia and anywhere in the Amazon basin. 'Couldn't you go?' Marchmont asked, occasionally, and 'Can we just send it?' or sometimes, 'Where is Elizabeth?'

'Will you be quiet a moment?' Kathleen asked him.

Then she told him that the dying man was putting the job in Marchmont's hands and shut up.

'He never stops playing the guitar,' the western writer told the hooker. 'What does he play?' What he didn't play was the wheel of the wagon is broken. Henry Wannamaker called at Marchmont's caravan at eleven in the morning and drove him to Heathrow airport, gave him tickets and funds.

'Do you know what it's all about?' he asked Claude.

'No.'

'Good – and good luck!'

Wannamaker watched the 707 take off to make certain the lad did not get off. Other members of the organisation made the bed and tidied up, putting the ladies wherever they required to be. With the bottles – three in different places for safety – of quinine in his keeping and with international medical support, Finbow's salesman felt he was travelling in medicine. He had noticed yesterday one of the sex aids black boxes had OXFAM stencilled on it. His passport and visa had been issued by WHO and overstamped with the House of Commons postmark, signed by David Murray, MD. He had sounded a very relaxed and not public school chap and he knew one of Marchmont's voices. 'That's Chick Murray!' he said and laughed. He himself played banjo. Either that or they were trying to disarm him. All the Indians on the plane, which was Air India, seemed to Marchmont to be carrying diamonds.

9

What an extraordinary thing, just to be sitting there thirty thousand feet above the Azores, as the captain had just told them. Even Essex was a long way to a dreamer. Like his parents, both writers, Marchmont had spent his life walking down the main street of Dodge City at High Noon, waiting for Lurch. He was being watched. Kathleen had dropped a hint that not everybody wanted Gerry Chapman healthy. Watch y' ass, son, his mother had told him. Now every time he looked at a passenger across the cabin he looked away. It was like a Spike Milligan gag.

'Are you Mr Marchmont?' the stewardess asked him. It was Niloufer, he now realised. The girl he slept with and who was a friend of Wannamaker, the chief constable, or something pretty big. 'You know I am, Niloufer – how did you get in here?' Gag. They knew when somebody had never flown before. Doctor David Murray joined him. It was his seat. The arrangement was that he took Marchmont all the way.

'I was waiting for you to speak and when you

98

didn't I thought – well, good security. But I think we're okay. Nice to meet you. Can we have drinks, miss?' It was not Niloufer. Murray did South American missions for WHO and occupational medicine at Westminster and for Brit contractors in the tropics. 'You met my wife at Gerry's – Elizabeth?' Marchy made a big remembrance. Of course! And what a lovely lady. That was Chapman's wife – or whoever was in the bathroom.

'We walked out of Colombia together.'

'You walked out of Colombia? I thought that was Gregory Peck?' He did George Sanders and it made the joke. 'Hovis were building fences for Bovril, two thousand miles of them, then suddenly the government changed.' Oh God, dear oh dear, what happened next? 'We walked to Uruguay, three Brits and one donkey, the usual cock-up. One carrier.' Not leprosy? He did Robert Mitchum and a few Mr Christians from Charles Laughton. Whatever the doctor related Marchmont thought was stand-up material. The rats stopped him gagging and he realised he was involved in a deal, big bucks. 'Elizabeth and I slept in copper miners' huts at twelve thousand feet with rats running along the roof beams above our faces – sometimes they fell on us. What's Gerry doing in Brazil?'

'He's hiding out till the big job comes up.'

Unaccountably this made the slim, steely, clean man with his serious chat, erupt into laughter. The reason he now showed to his young listener; it was that morning's *Telegraph* with THE GERRY CHAPMAN STORY CONTINUES as a headline and under it – *Is he smuggling rain forests and if so who sent the mosquito?*

'That's pretty funny stuff, isn't it?' Marchmont said. He was terrified again. And where did Murray come into the list? 'I am based normally at St Thomas's, but they rent us out, you know, like film stars. There's not a lot of money in it but satisfaction, I suppose. I control the Prime Minister's bowels.' Marchmont wanted to ask about the IRA. 'Do you know Ruby?' he said, out of the blue.

'No,' said David, with the promptness of a man who finds it easier to remember the girls he doesn't know. They landed in Nassau, New Providence Island, and then were headed across the Caribbean. At Nassau, the men Marchy and Kathleen had called Ronald Lacey and Harry Towb boarded the aircraft and sat unseen in tourist. The king was dying. Harry displayed the *Nassau Tribune* with a fine figure of Sir Etienne Dupuch in the braided uniform of Knight Commander of the Order of St Gregory the Great, just conferred by Pope Pius, one foot raised on a stone garden sculpture in back of the Dupuch family home at Camperdown – where they, Etienne being editor and proprietor of the famous class-racist-crusading *Tribune*, had entertained the Duke of Windsor and the Duchess, an American, while he was Governor of the Bahamas during World War 2. The two villains wore the whole thing on their laps as Colditz escapees were forced to turn sandbags into female skirts.

A Rolls Royce ambulance with four out-riders on bikes as big and shiny as destroyers, rushed Marchmont from the Rio Aeroporto to the wrong hospitalo.

David, who knew it, sat patiently while the mistake was applauded and put right, finally landing them in an isolation hut behind a methane sewage gas works where the shadow of Gerry Chapman lay comatose. The fat Olly Hardy conniver of Gerry's in the Country looked like the rejected portrait of Churchill at eighty.

'What's happened to him?' Marchmont whispered. The doctor who could speak a bit of English and looked, Marchy felt instantly, like Lee Montagu, a bit Chinese, never out of work, told him it was the anti-malaria medication, now to be put right. David mentioned a few medical things to which the Mexican nodded. Dr Murray then said briefly: 'The clots have had him on short-wave hyper-pyrexia, think of a bit of meat in a coil of wire – it kills the germ just before it kills the meat, if you don't drink, for instance, or fuck women.' The bilingual doctor nodded again.

By seven in the evening Gerry was comfortable and talking and had got the grapes. It did not surprise the tally boy to discover that the villain and the doctor in the Houses of Parliament knew each other; pre-armed that Elizabeth was in fact the international doctor's wife. 'Elizabeth couldn't come but sends her love,' David told the patient who moved his eyelids. 'She has not broken her cover,' David added. This seemed to have been accepted and David Murray gave the third party a side-glance as a security screen; can I speak? got the nod. David spoke. 'Liz is running in the city as a Bank of England messenger. I understand you have everything. There's somebody has to be knocked out – that should be supervised. Well, for the Red Cross. Presumably you have a list train driver – good. Good. Good.' David said good three or four times and oh? even though Oliver Hardy appeared to say nothing. Then Marchy noticed that the doctor's skilled hand was resting on the famous smuggler's knee, through the bed cover. Marchmont had played it himself, it was one of his para-normal tricks on electric-clock-crazy housewives. You had to have a third person.

An incredibly fearsome creole nurse came in holding what Marchy thought was a head-hunter's knife. 'You get out soon!' Then she grinned with two teeth missing and put the telephone back on its hook – an efficient point not missed by the three. Gerry spoke properly for the first time. 'Everything is in good hands, David.' And he smiled faintly, grateful for the Claude Marchmonts of this world, *di innocenti*. 'Why are you here, David?' Marchmont asked, when Chapman appeared to be asleep and they were getting ready to leave, nicking souvenirs. 'There's been a takeover bid,' said the doctor. 'I am conveyancing.' From the bed and without opening his eyes, the grand old man of Avenue Foch torture chambers said: 'It won't affect your job, Marchmont.'

'Oh, I see.' He didn't see. Who could see takeover bids for crimes? Claude's employer knew how little Claude understood. 'You get a bigger car. You get ten thousand dollars anywhere you want it. You get married to Kathleen Finbow. Finis.'

'Can I go home now?' said Marchy; say goodnight Gracy voice. They laughed and David said: 'What guitar does your dad play? Folk or steel?' Malcolm played steel. 'Is he a good reader – music?' Malcolm

102

is a slow reader but a good memoriser, once learned. Gerry Chapman said, 'He doesn't play tunes. He plays riffs. He plays extempore, David. Very good when he's good, when he's not being listened to. Now fuck off – have some girls. Rio girls have their own taxi rank.' In a taxi to the San Francisco Hotel, Marchmont explained to the doctor, finding himself in command of a subject for the first time. His old man plays guitar like sculptors sculpt. Some sculptors find their inspiration in their raw material. 'Diane the sculptor from Chiswick does that – there was a piece in *Punch*. Dad took her up to the quarry at – that little county, Rutland – and a rock fell on her. That's what Malcolm does with his Gibson – he crashes a few chords and riffs and from it recognises maybe one phrase. You take like – by my bedside every night – *Misty*? *Misty* is the same as Ellington's *Sophisticated Lady*? Ba ba barm . . . !' Marchy was whistling it, the girl driver with her little window open was half-turned to the music, when David said: 'That wasn't your dad with the sculptor, that was Horace. Horace Spurgeon Fenton. Sorry!' Marchmont thought around inside his muddled head, it was like a haunted rehearsal room. Some people said Horace was his real father, that Tres and Rosie were the same person.

'How did you get his caravan?' David the doctor said, quietly, as if giving him something to go by. Alice was the one they all thought that Horace was going to marry, when he was free. Alice Finbow, Albert's tax man's daughter, married Albert when she was really in love with the author and working as a librarian in Luton. 'Well, it doesn't matter,' Marchy said. Who is

103

going to sleep with the driver . . . ? And if not, the smell of methane gas had gone. 'He gives me diamonds,' Marchmont said, about Horace.

That night in Rio the doctor and the tally boy had a cabaret supper and chatted up two girls from Buffalo at the bar, one of whom said to Marchmont, much later on, in her room where she felt she had more control, which she had, 'You fall in love with the very kind of girl who could never possibly have anything in the whole world to do with you! C'marn!'

She was explaining the Catholic to him and holding one of his fingers in case she fell asleep and yielded. Years later, too later, in some unleavable relationship and from a Chicago address a letter arrived to Marchy through Amnesty International, London, asking him to help her to come over and signed 'Your finger friend'. Marchmont was still alive, as in aspic. 'You lost your five hundred at Clophill?' David told Marchmont a few days later, back at the aeroporto where they were parting, David to walk into the badlands, Marchy going home. He remembered the girl who took his money walking out of Poland, the strangled geese. 'Yes, that was a very good story – I've forgotten her name. She's one of ours – Reiner radioed ahead and she was on the lookout. They pay well, but they always get back what they can if you digress – or even if you don't. My World Health lot are like that, and film companies – I know Larry Harvey was held in his Garden of Allah hotel hut by force until he had settled a contract reduction through MCA with Harry Cohen on the phone. You know about Larry and Joan? Anyway, it wasn't that. It was money. Where do you keep your diamonds?'

Without meaning to, Marchy's hand went to his flies and came back again and the Westminster doctor, spy, walker, appeared not to have noticed – he had set it up – and said did Marchy realise that he, David, had a bullet-proof diplomatic bag. David Murray had timed this information to the moment when the customs panic sets in, even with ordinarily brave tourists. He laughed at Marchmont's eyebrows and dance contortions and five, five, five, shit – fifty thousand pounds there! He touched his balls. David said: 'Forget it. You look as though you don't know whether to get your cock out or do it down your leg.' At the boarding gate at parting they were pointing to each other, like accusing friends. When Doctor Murray vanished Marchmont knew that he had been murdered and buried. As he knew everything else, David had told Marchmont that most official people going to investigate anything in the corrupt up-rivers got murdered and not investigated further. Rats on the beams falling on the faces. Women in Brighton mourned David and women in Valparaiso and Hamburg and the new city in the Midlands where he had done his GP. Murray was survived by Elizabeth, his wife.

10

Kathleen came home with her new face. Everything was in hazard because of Gerry's mosquito in Brazil. That was not just lying low for Gerry, that was a connection to oil through Reiner Wertzen's gas and part of multi-purpose funding. In the nick of time Kathleen and Elizabeth bought the already researched farm at Akeley, later famous for its empty money packaging and lack of fingerprints.

'I'm worried about David,' Elizabeth said. They had heard nothing for forty-eight hours and Pinnochio was not back either. 'Well, I'll tell you something – put your gloves on – David always told me, when he was relaxed,' said Kathleen, meaning in bed, they did not hedge about the cross-pollination of the Gerry Chapman clan, 'if I'm murdered in Brazil, don't believe it.' With their gloves on they set about cleaning the farmhouse up, making it habitable for the necessary three days of occupation following the hold-up. Kathleen sang, I don't want to play in your yard and Elizabeth was in love with her. Her depressions concerned that boy who had his tea and sat down and made a will. Kathleen saw her crying and held her, kissed her. They arranged to spend the night together in Marchmont's caravan at Hermitage Park, nesting several birds of emotion, for their own boy might come back from his travels and need them. Being nervous and having had his car blown up by presumably the IRA in search of Ruby, Marchmont was rich in planned survival tricks, one of which was to telephone the airline about the flight he had booked on and warn them a bomb had been placed on it.

'That's clever,' Elizabeth said. 'I can see the point of that. Special searching!'

'But not only that, my dear – he then misses that flight and goes for the next available, like it might be from standby.' To Elizabeth, gang leader's mistress and wife of a top go-between, this was brilliant thinking. More so when she recollected, lying with her arms and legs around her friend in the tally boy's bed, that the device would explain why David was late finding him aboard the wrong plane at the wrong time. As if in answer to the love and concern melting between them, what was happening now? came the radio news of a bomb warning in Rio this afternoon resulting in the finding of the bomb and arrest of four West Bank motivated terrorists working for Irak.

'I-R-A ---K?' said Elizabeth. 'With a doctor's handwriting in code and decode and scrambled – you know. Do you realise that Marchmont is a hero again?' They finished making love, then checked on flights to the UK from Rio and reckoned the boy would be home by dawn, which he was. In the meantime they had turned over his van and found no diamonds but instead some of his gems of wisdom to the press.

Dear Mr Editor,
    I have just seen a red woodpecker. It is bright red at the bottom of its belly, pink at the breast and a kind of dark and light striped back and head with a tuft. I think it was a tuft. My caravan window is steamy. Before this I have seen two woodpeckers, both green, one walking across my father's lawn at Billericay and one on Hampstead Heath, going like a pneumatic drill. This one today, the red one, was holding itself upright on the thin crooked trunk of an ancient wild apple tree and pecking slowly. I think the reason your paper is full of bad news is that this country and others should exchange governments and do away with sovereignty and nationalism and the price of happiness and peace would be affordable. I live in Hitchin. Nobody wants to invade Hitchin. Yrs: Marchmont.

'They never get used,' Kathleen told Elizabeth.
    'He mixes his subjects.' But no, Marchmont won't have that, the Irish rose explained. The subject always is the same – Marchmont. 'Climbs mountains,' Elizabeth said, nodding her head slowly in the American rock age fashion. She told Kathleen to make herself convalescent and not sure she would live, still, but Marchmont burst in looking for his car. 'What's happened to my Rover? Where is my car? I said don't move it! Where the hell is it? Hello, Elizabeth – ' but his stare at the one he loved and

was going to marry on October 31st was angry and accusing. He did not see the rather fetchingly brutal thing the surgery had done to the soft Irish forehead, a kind of James Cagney thrust that Irish faces can revert to and what had kept Elizabeth gasping and panting and sobbing every time it moved on her.

'I put it into Fletcher's for servicing and safety – I told them to leave my blood on the dashboard for you.' He said, 'Oh, thank God!' and clasped her nearly naked body to him as if it were a Rover. 'We've been going through some of your letters,' Elizabeth told him and he did his Jack Benny – 'Never mention my letters to Kathleen – especially a packet of one!' Kathleen said she was really sorry about that and it reminded her that Horace and Tres had rung from Jersey and the news was that Alice Finbow, Kathleen's cousin by marriage to Eric, had won a million pounds on the pools and lived in Hillingdon, Middlesex. There was a strong mixed feeling about the futures in relation to pasts, of the legacy of sorrows left by Albert, that persisted, now through-out the tapping of Flossie from across the path and the discreet inquiry by the noddy policeman on his quiet Velocette and until Elizabeth had exchanged final information on the big job and brought Marchy up-to-date on the farm, a strong feeling that Alice would marry Horace at last. All it ever needed was money.

'Tres needs somebody younger now,' Kathleen said, fairly. Tres herself was old enough to want a boy. Elizabeth had to get back to South Mymms and took Kathleen's car, an MG, dates were made and promises and there you go.

* * *

109

'I used to believe that Gerry murdered Eric for love of me, which is a compliment,' said Kathleen to the gathering, 'but I don't think that now, do I, Gerry?' Gerry Chapman shook his head. He could not speak yet, but sat at the big council chamber like a listening judge. All were not present yet and gossip had the floor. 'Ah sure, in the army you think everybody that dies is a casualty,' she explained, her hand on March- mont's. Marchmont was blindfolded, but smoking and relaxed. She said, 'The going of Eric was inevi- table, right up his what-d'you-call-it, tying himself aboard with a bow line just long enough to drown him overboard upside down!' The laughter was abundant and the man who looked like John Junkin the actor, always propping up the bar at Gerry's, reminded them of Eric Finbow's first mad voyage from Burnham round to Leigh, single-handed, after selling their house and buying the boat from a man in a pub and unable to put up the sails on his own. 'He had to shit holding a box,' Kathleen told them. 'But then when the coast cutter found him he said he was okay and then called, as they went, which way is London!'

'I must speak,' said Gerry, holding his throat. The malaria had affected it. 'The dancing I remember, you and Eric, exotic dancers, like George Raft – Ballet Rambert stuff. Remember Sylvia dancing naked at the Savoy every night and pretending she was wear- ing a body-stocking! Limbo dancing. Then one night she come home and made her cocoa, still half naked and Horace, in the next room, came in and cooked one of his stinking fry-ups and was overcome with passion, picked her up, six feet of her nearly, and carried her into her room and threw her onto the bed and himself on top – '

'God almighty he'd been wanting to do it for a year, putting up with her cats and wounded pigeons – she used to make him climb chimneys – and he got the wrong night! I don't mind, Horace, she told him, but you've got the wrong week!' Albert was proud of Horace, added Kathleen.

Marchmont put in, 'And he went back to cooking his fucking chitterlings!' Then he said, 'Who's that?' Because he was blind and could not see the Colonel had just entered with another German, both saying minimum things – 'Reiner and Otto are with us,' Kathleen whispered to her chief salesman. The shop had been closed by the police, awaiting a magistrates' decision on the confiscated sex aids. Browning and the girls and young Gringo were on full abeyance pay – at Butlins in Clacton, where the season was peaking with the heat wave, August 14 coming up.

Kathleen touched Marchmont's long nose and he stood up, unable to see but fully confident, rapped the table with his glass of whisky, slopping it. 'Fuck. Sorry – welcome everybody. I'm on a bit of a blind, as you can see – ' Kathleen cut across the laughter with her new battered aggression: 'Cut out the jokes, Claude – we have a lot to do.' Elizabeth came in wearing motorbike clothes and a crash helmet, now wrenching it off to show her cropped boy's hair, the messenger. 'Have I missed anything?' Nobody answered her; Marchmont continued. 'I am CO now – Gerry's put me in charge. I know the job, I don't know the details. The reason is, I sing. People who sing get nailed to the floor – right, Paul?' Paul

111

Kraynes nodded – a smart kid in railway uniform. Everyone there was dressed for the night. Said Marchy:

'There will be no guns. There will be truncheons. There will be shoulder holsters – empty, but nobody knows that except the jury – sorry!'

Gerry Chapman spoke: 'I don't mind a joke, Marchy. Go through the jobs using actors' names, Alfie Bass and Leo and so on. You don't need your eyes – ' Marchmont was groping for his notes, 'All right, Alfie, put your hand up, thank you, you and Harry – Harry? – you are on the signal with a red lens to clamp over the green, Harry helping. Gloves of course. Bill – fergit name, Bootsie and Snudge – you and Junkin in the driving cab when it stops at the red, make ugly noises, hit Pat on the head hard – Pat?'

'Present,' said Pat.

Marchmont hesitated. 'I'm not sure what you do with the real driver?'

'Pat is the real driver,' Kathleen said.

There was a commotion, everybody nervous, saying so, calling for correction, saying: 'That should not have been mentioned – that fucks it.' The genuine train staff on the villain list should not be identifiable at any stage. Kathleen said: 'I'm sorry, Gerry.' Gerry said: 'All right. We have a flaw. Carry on, Marchy – the mail van?'

'Six in the mail van,' Marchmont said. 'Maddern, Dwyer, Slater, Gregson, Lacey – Lacey – '

'McKern,' said Gerry. 'All hands have been raised, Marchmont. Now the Guard's van and security –

112

three people to deal with, one armed or with access – '

'Okay,' said Marchmont. What am I doing here, mummy? 'We have a chemist, qualified, with weak ammonia, psssh psssh pssh, like that, we will exterminate! Don't hit anybody too hard, you might meet them coming back – '

The train robbers laughed and clapped and drank and smoked and enjoyed it more than they would the real thing. Half their takings went to charities and not too much to Great Ormond Street more than little ones and so on.

'What about me?'

'Is that Monty? Lee? You're up on the bank, mate, lookout. You've got a whistle. There's Kathleen and Elizabeth with a red, half a mile both ways in case something comes – it shouldn't. I'm in the signal box at Salcey Forest – '

'You're fucking not,' Gerry said.

'Don't be daft, Marchy!' said Kathleen.

Chelsea Ted, last to speak, for a good reason – he was the last involved, he was the tractor driver waiting for the bags – leaned over and pulled Pinnochio's nose. Marchmont swung out at him and punched Kathleen in the face, she went down with her chair and her drink and came up bleeding again. 'All right,' she said, 'so we're going to get married.'

It went off quite well. Maps were projected. Gerry thanked Marchmont and the Germans joined them. Reiner was always a little suspicious of humour and therefore of Marchmont, though he valued him. 'This is Otto,' he explained to our lad. 'Otto Todt – of the Todt Organisation. They have made a takeover bid

113

through David but he has gone missing with a hundred thousand dollars.'

'Not a hundred thousand dollars?' said Marchy.

'It's only a five percent advance – we are talking about millions on this TPO – it's used notes for burning.' Marchmont knew that. It was his tip-off.

'Why don't they burn them in Liverpool?' Kathleen put the question to elicit: they don't come from Liverpool, they come from the whole country, shovelled into the Euston line all the way down, ten sorters sorting as they also dealt with regional mail, hooks on the wagons picking up and dropping off, like a movie. Buster Keaton got picked up once and dropped into a net. The tractor and trailer would go across country from Salcey Forest to the remote farm at Akeley and get resorted. After that Marchmont was allowed to take off his blindfold and play bar billiards.

'I never got to know what happens after the farm – it won't be safe on the roads,' Marchy said. Kathie lit him a ciggie. This was the mistake.

He was not told.

'It's what script writers call a clever device,' Kathleen said. 'You ask your old man.'

'You know what Malcolm said about that french letter? After they'd taken the girls home from the Studio Club to Kilburn – Little Venice – Lords – Maids something – '

'I know her. Clare. Albert used her in his space capsule once, on promotions – I didn't know she was on the game, but of course she was, who wasn't with Horace and Albert?'

'Believe in God, my dad told him, but wear this

114

anyway!' They laughed together at their common heritage. At the brothel at Bush End Ruby waited up with television news for them. A white man had been rumoured living with the Aranguana pygmies in the central Andes, painting his body and co-habiting and killing animals for food – he could speak no English.

'He learnt that quickly,' Marchmont commented.

There was a note of hope there and Kathleen telephoned Gerry's bedroom at the Lodge and asked to talk to Elizabeth. 'I'll get the boys to rescue him,' Gerry Chapman promised. It's not the money. She repeated it in bed and Marchy could feel the nails coming through the spring mattress of the leaning luxury plywood Berkeley three-quarters-size fitted bed. She told him that David was researching the Amazon for a new and startling aphrodisiac which would be provided by the DHSS, where needed.

11

The girl taxi driver waiting outside for him in the morning – un-ordered – gave him the spark. 'I had to see you, please. I am breaking up.' She was foreign, she was Greek and she seemed to know him or have heard of him. She was his sister-in-law, but Marchmont did not find this out until almost too late. She told him of meeting George in Rome where she had a baby by a Vatican priest and could not claim maintenance.

'I knew a girl like that,' Marchmont told her. He sat beside her in the bright but old London taxi. He had to go out to Slacey Museum Farm where the police were asking for his assistance in another agricultural relic robbery. 'I was a famous girl in the London papers for six weeks on the front page – The Maid of Athens. It was a famous breach-of-promise case I brought against the officer who seduced me in Athens and deserted me to come back and marry a debutante of a titled family – '

'Look out!'

She did a double swerve – the Athens slalom – and

116

did not stop talking. Judge Jeffreys had taken the case and had ordered that the girl should be given time to master the English language and conduct her own case, face her own seducer and his rotten millions. It had emerged that the girl was a hero.

'I'm a hero,' Marchmont informed her. 'I helped a chap in a car accident and I saved a jet full of passengers – I may do more.'

'I know,' she said. 'I know, Marchy! You are very lovely. I am telling George all this time to bring our problem to you – you see, during the civil war in Greece after the Germans had gone and the British were handing us over to the Junta colonels, my papa lost all his lands and went into a concentration camp with the labour party. The left was not needed once the Russians had died for us – I escaped to England and won my case. I had three thousand pounds award but it went nowhere and I went to Rome and advertised in the *Daily American* – see here – '

'Careful!'

She pulled a newspaper cutting out of her breast. Marchmont began to realise she must have been preparing for somebody to come along and listen. 'Greek young lady will take you shopping and so on. Familiar.' Marchy smiled. 'They really printed this?' She stopped the taxi. She was lost. 'And then you fell in love with this George character?' He looked around him. They were still in Hitchin. 'Let me have the wheel – we need to be in Codicote.' Driving her then, he was able to see her body and her legs.

'Where are you living?'

'Oh. I don't know.' Her eyes welled. 'I hope to stay with you tonight? Please? George has not

117

touched me for a hundred-and-one nights.' Let's not make it two, he thought. But he said: 'Have you thought of going to marriage guidance?' Or learning German? 'I went to prison for stabbing my girl friend,' he said, which seemed to balance their backgrounds. 'Yes, I heard about that, Marchy.' She put a hand on his, on the wheel. He was alarmed to see that she was wearing gloves. This was supposed to be a day off.

'Claude!' The Slacey farmyard had three police cars in it and Ross's little scruffy Traveller – she waved him down. Gone was the cowboy outfit, she now wore country tweeds and a 1925 cloche hat; this was antiques day. She had telephoned Kathleen at the brothel and then at the shop and then at a hairdressers, friendly people passing her on. 'There's some lovely old brasses here – and a china horse! I must have it – hello, Anna.' Marchmont was about to introduce them but did not know the girl's name yet. He did not butt in but bided his time until he had discovered that this was George's Anna, the leavable marriage, the marriage never visited. Marchy was best man at the wedding in Dorking, a long time ago. He let it all fall into place without Anna ever discovering his dereliction. It was one of his gifts.

Gamble was there and glad to see Marchmont. 'I had them send for you, Mr Marchmont – Vicky had a bright idea about these agricultural museum robberies. Tell him, Vicky – This is Victoria Plum,' he added to Ross and Anna. 'Hello, Marchmont!' came a cry or two, from the police. 'I'm Sid, I'm Albert's friend!' Of course he was. Know Albert, know every-body. 'I tell you what I think might be happening,' said the WPC. Marchy let her take him into the Victorian parlour of the lovely relic building. Men of eighty would feel they had come home.

It was the young policewoman's quite bright idea that some crank was surrounding himself with the farming equipment of early century England in order to farm as his ancestors had farmed. 'He has now taken a tractor and its trailer – Massey Ferguson 1917. He has a ploughshare and its leathers for a horse to pull. Miss Fere! Mr Bellwether! Can you come – this is Marchmont.' Marchmont shook hands with the nucleus of the Slacey Farm Collection members, all oddly period. They remembered him at the farm auctions, working for Rumbelows. 'We've lost our lovely windmill and the butter-making machine and oh, wind-up gramophones and treadle sewing machines and a harrow and seeder and thresher – not everything. If we have two, he only takes one. If we have one – he takes it.' This was Miss Fere, the secretary.

'It might be a she,' said the cowboy writer, hands on her hips.

Marchmont said to Ackroyd; that was Vicky's real name: 'You might be right. There's a lot of very nice little farms out there in the – well, you take Ashwell and Morden and Shepreth and along the Icknield and that.' Very nice being able to talk native some-times. Proud came over and nodded at Marchy. 'Is Kathleen – Mrs Finbow at home? She had an acci-dent.' Marchmont brought him up to date and saw him get his driver and leave. The back of the police car was stacked up with returned evidence.

Gamble came to the point *vis a vis* the lad: 'You used to pole around the farms for the auctioneers – can you remember any remote farm that looked a bit say – old-fashioned? Lace curtains, bloomers on the line, a donkey?' Gamble overtook his imagination and dried up.

'I tell you what I'll do. I'll think about it, Mr Gamble.' That was Albert talking. Trouble was, what did Albert think when he thought about it?

Ross joined in, with a sudden enthusiasm. 'There's a nice little farm over at Akeley, near Buckingham, for sale, Claude – how much money have you got? I've been looking around – we could have horses. I'm his mother,' she told the police, as if he was her passport. To blur the name Akeley he made a few intelligent inquiries. Is the stolen machinery in working condition? Ray Bellwether, a man with an asian dandelion of white hair, told them it was in perfect working order for their numerous open days for the public. 'That's what we're here for, every weekend, right through summer and winter – we have Morris Dancers and lace-makers and a Maypole, there's a print shop and a weaving shed and we're geared for Chilton cheese and parma, with live pigs when they're in litter,' said Miss Fere.

'We'll have a look at Akeley,' said Gamble. The Chief Inspector had caught panic in the tally boy's manner and pinned it to the cause. Marchmont meanwhile was slotting Anna's and George's relationship problem into his Finbow marriage repair clinic. It would be interesting to see what David brought back from the dark continent. Driving her back he could see her in bed with George, both with vibrators and extended french letters, with magic lettuce cock-raiser sandwiches. Backed by the DHSS. 'You should be allowed to step off the kerb with that,' the chairman of the Greater London Council had told Albert in one of the Arabian Albert legends. Move the clock forward one second, if not, why are we here? The actors asked the actors asked the actors. How salutary then to come home and find someone as real life as Lorel waiting with the vicar in the caravan park. She was an ungainly child of about fifteen at that stage and her mental block of autism had ravaged her appearance and persona. Her voice was loud and coarse by contact with the loud and coarse and her eyes starved – for everything. 'Mummy!' she croaked. 'Have you got my Guinness! Have you got my cigarettes? Oh, Christ, who are these silly buggers? All staring!'

'I found her sitting on the caravan steps – her name is on her dress tab. We've been having a nice little chat, haven't we, Lorel?'

'Is he a real vicar?' she asked Ross. The hospital at Shenley had a number of vicars. 'You are a damn nuisance, Lorel. I told you never follow me! You could get murdered. How did you get here?'

'I hitch-hiked in three lorries and the last one made me get out. Then I got a bus – which is my brother?'

Marchmont raised his hand, timidly. Rather frighteningly he saw signs of himself in this creature and always had. She was all the bad things in a family without any social skin. Kathleen and Anna were watchers, first night audience. It was the side of the

Albert show few broads ever got into. Horace seemed to be able to deal with it and so did Malcolm; the oldies, touched with a necessary madness themselves; likewise the cowboy. 'Have you got testicles under your bottom, vicar?' Lorel asked at some stage of the supper in the van. 'Yes, I suppose I have, child,' he said. 'Haven't you looked?' she said. And when Ross asked Marchmont (crying to get away before the Irish rose went off him for life): 'Would you like some beans, Claude?' he said, 'No thanks, I've just farted.' What a fortunate joke, what a cross-culture joke at that tense moment with everybody laughing for it was funny through all the layers, and unacceptable. 'You're bloody rude you are,' his sister told him, but she loved it. Nurses said things like that to her. Arnold Peck found the encounter refreshing. He told a rude joke about Boadicea, his wife, and how she got her nick-name. Lorel was free and unbound and therefore universal; reached and was reachable.

'We're going to live on a farm,' her mother told her. Ranch was in her mind, always. She never got it. And did George know where his lady was? That is important in a tribe. 'He's a photographer,' Anna explained to the assembly. All the clowns fell silent. Latish, though still daylight, Marchmont got up to let the vicar out, but held him at the door to make an announcement.

'Has anybody ever heard of a chain of good class stores throughout the country, throughout the world, called, roll of drums, Wonderful Things!'

'What sort of wonderful things?' Anna asked.

'Don't interrupt him,' said Kathleen.

'What it is is,' said the tally boy, 'it's a place where you can buy happiness – part of it – no listen – part of it is goodies, nice things to buy and wear and use. Part is a love shop – that's an over-eighteen part perhaps. I don't know yet. If we want social approval and subsidy, clinic status for instance, there may be some statutory restrictions. But we sell sex aids, sex hints, sex everything – it's like Harrods with sex. For resident singles and couples to volunteer we shall be like Gerry's in the Country – '

Ross said, 'You're talking about the good old western style brothel, you're talking about the movie, what was it? The – '

The Hottest Little Whorehouse in Texas,' said the Reverend Peck.

'Wonderful Things is a very nice name for a chain.' Kathleen nodded her rock age head again, everybody agreeing. 'You and George could give it a fling,' Ross told Anna. Lorel was not particularly interested. Kathleen liked it because Finbow's was living in the half-dark of a too-early decade. It would put the tally and sex business in a sunnier spectrum. One needed to play slaves and masters and to play puritans and to play *Northanger Abbey.* Horace had written a movie for Renown called *The Victorian County* in which cars and telephones were left at the gate. This thought was abroad and Ross said to Kathleen, 'You're a Finbow, aren't you? Alice is a Finbow.' No, Alice is still Mrs Argyle and Tres is still Mrs Bluett, though both are widowed they are only widowed by Horace Spurgeon Fenton – or so it seemed.

Outside in the park there were calling voices and

the kicking of a motor bike and the sound of a deep trombone.

'That's the Monty Sunshine band,' said the reverend. 'Or part of it – Tony the trumpet is across the way at Perdido and Rod Mason you can hear – sorry, Marchmont?'

'Tony Bagot is string bass and Rod is trumpet – he hit Monty with his pint mug when he was drunk and got the sack. That's why he's here tonight – ' then he did his Snozzle Durante delayed take, hand to ear, long nose quivering ' – that's not a trumpet – that's a trombone!' The band had been playing in Rio de Janeiro and David the doctor had sat in on banjo, a thing he carried through jungles.

'Can I ring George?' Anna asked, familiarly.

They smiled at each other and at themselves and at money and sex and so forth. Now Kathleen was able to explain, as an Albert watcher: 'She didn't find George in Rome. She found Horace in Rome writing movies. She got him out of a tangle with an American journalist girl, Theda Plowright, who was pregnant by a mafia chap and used Horace to get drugs, then took an overdose, Horace running down the mountain, Monte Mario, late one Sunday night to find her still alive and washing up. Anna got him out safely and entrusted him with her Maid of Athens dossier – the complete press cuttings – royalty were involved – to try to get it published as a book. Horace took it to his publisher who raved about it – then Horace lost it!'

'Where did he lose it?'

'On his desk! You know! She tried to get to him but then he was shacked up with Maggie who wouldn't let anybody get near him for five years and

124

then went to Brussels. Anna's coming back. That dossier would prove Anna's land rights in Greece under the democracy and make them rich! Ssssh!'

'Is George all right, dear,' asked Ross. Her sons were always all right. It was a perfect family for writers, never together, Horace married lifelong to his first sweetheart, Evelyn May Overton, short, blonde, pretty and now cleaning offices in Welwyn Garden City, though still doing Horace's laundry on the machine provided by George and Peter and Lee and their advertising jobs, lots of buckshee domestic tally-ware which they photographed with pretty models – that's where Greek Anna had come from. Horace brought her back for them. If a girl can skip mentioning a couple of necessary lays en route, she will.

Ross phoned the mental hospital and promised to bring Lorel back tomorrow, George was driving north for another reunion with Anna and we are returning with Marchmont and Kathleen to bad news. Gerry has got cancer of the throat. Soon they all had it, because that is what cancer is; everybody on the slip road away from day calendars.

Meanwhile Malcolm Marchmont was scriptwriting in Billericay. Malcolm was non-resident illegal husband to Ross as Evelyn was legal wife to Horace Fenton. They had four girls and a boy. For Marchmont life was a very fragile game of draughts and everything went in threes. In the late, dark evening on Thursday the 14th of August, a telephone engineer up a pole with earphones on, shouted down to his mate: 'Charlie! We've got a blow-out on number six for sausages – we need a new one and quick!'

Number six for sausages, one may gather, was

Marchmont the master-mind's code for Pat the train driver, who had been replaced at the last moment. Did this have anything to do with blowing the gaff at the Lodge – Kathleen's flaw? Marchy could not go to Gerry. Later a line work-gang of thirteen figures, two female, made a quick decision. It was on and they would have to hit the driver.

'Not if he's frightened,' said Marchmont. 'Only if he's brave.'

'Permission to speak, sir?' This was a Clive Dunn. 'If it so happens that Mr Chapman does not want to continue but is giving it to Jerry, other Jerry, do we withdraw? Otherwise we are going to have two lots.' Nobody replied to this, it was known that two British Railway open lorries were to be standing side by side in the Salcey Forest timber works clearing and that at twelve minutes past two o'clock in the morning, Marchmont would stand in front of them and point his finger at one of them. One was the Gerry Chapman lorry and the other was the Reiner Wertzen gang of gas pipe layers. Whichever one went it would be an even split.

12

Marchmont kept them guessing for a little amusing warm-up, standing by himself in the clearing as if to take a picture of the two gangs. Each gang was spread around the bonnet of their BR lorry, the scene lit by a very high cloud-ceiling of diffused moonlight. They were all dressed for the kill and nervous. If a car with headlights sped past they ducked their faces and became two piles of tinder and rubbish. Marchmont could not tell which was the female coefficient. There was silence until the tally boy had finished watching his wrist, upon which there was no timepiece, as everybody knew, since warm-ups and his long nose and eyebrows had become familiar.

'All right,' he told them, relaxing now. 'It's over the top. What does that mean?'

'You,' Kathleen said.

Laughter. Just the optimum release. Far diesels wailed. Marchmont now raised his hand to point, then turned slowly around away from them and into the trees and away from them at the lane and slowly coming back, the wheel of chance, to point at the gas men.

'Oh Fuck and Jesus Christ!' said Ruby. She had thought with this one big job she would get the bhoys off her back. She had spent two weeks dressed as a man and feigning pissing standing up. Pssssssssss. Doing it in her sleep now and waking up with a wet bed.

'There is to be no wasting time,' Marchmont said.

He watched the Reiner Wertzen lorry drive one way and the Gerry Chapman lorry the other. For the next day or two the losers were to make themselves apparent for alibis, for the jury, but not conspicuous. They were not to play guitars outside Scotland Yard.

Doctor David Murray was holding the Horace Fenton novel and about to read it to a couple of chums on the terrace overlooking the Thames in the well-known place. 'Before you start, David, do you mind if I have a good old scream? Then I won't interrupt you – Margaret?' She nodded, 'Yes, have one for me.' Because the roving *agent provocateur* appeared to be looking at the world from an iron mask; purple dye had been painted over his face in horizontal stripes, zebra stripes, his hair shaven back in a saucer and painted scarlet, both ears tipped with luminous white. He looked and had been told so several times, as though he had just got back from San Francisco. 'Let me read this – as a prediction of this morning's blatts it's quite uncanny . . .' It was an extract, parenthetical from the busy life of the author's first person, giving an historical immediacy instantly believable today – the House had been in uproar.

128

Whatever publicity Albert might have achieved the next day fell quite flat for there had been a mail train robbery involving millions of pounds and the newspapers were filled with it, each edition trying to cap the last with the amount involved. There was a jubilant, public-holiday feeling everywhere as the hold-up took the place of the weather between total strangers. Even Tres was smiling as the telecasts came over. For us, particularly, living between the cracks of a weekly and monthly and quarterly ordered society, there was a feeling of achievement; that the Spanish Main was still there and some of the gold had come to us night people at last instead of to them. It was a blow against the solicitors, the seven-day makers. It was a battle in a war that we could understand. It was crime without a knighthood in mind.

It was the 6th of August, 1963.

'But that's very odd,' Margaret Seething said. 'Or almost very odd. That was ten days ago – when did the book come out? Let me see, David – Seckers published it, always unusual, mock-ordinary. David Cook and so on – oh, I see, fifty-nine. That's an unusual prescience for Horace Fenton.' David Murray laughed and his face looked like a spinning one-arm-bandit. He explained that Albert's adventures had been inspired at that moment by young Marchmont working on the TPO. Youth training. 'The date was just a future stab with George Orwell,' said Edward Heath, a bucolic musical man. 'Are we to meet him – not Horace, this young hero?' asked Margaret.

'Not half,' the minister said. 'He saved my life and two hundred more – we're giving him a lunch.'

'That is good,' said the lady. Then, chewing a bit, 'Though I'm not sure!' Then she screamed and said: 'For God's sake don't laugh, David!' After leaving Marchmont at the Rio aeroporto, the doctor had flown to Ecuador to distribute a million dollars in crudos to the immigrant peon labour, the object being to release them from bondage and freak out an unpopular government – unpopular in Washington.

'Reiner told me you took a hundred thousand,' Marchmont told Murray, later. 'For myself, I suppose? South Africans say things like that.' Marchmont thought that Reiner was American – from top secret Chicksands. 'He's a mercenary,' David said. 'That means neutral – they'll kill anybody,' said Marchy. Then he said, 'What's the time?' The doctor told him he was all right for time. They were now sitting in the hot steamy jacuzzi at Sticks In The Country, Manny the masseur working on the painted man's bizarre mural. It was not ordinary paint or ordinary dye. 'It's from that big purple vegetable the Greeks use a lot – like an outsize testicle,' David said. The secret was in the fixer.

'You still can't remember the name of the fixer?' asked Manny. But he knew deep down this man would die behind his stripes. A telephone bell crackled for David. Marchmont took a towel and got up and went for it.

'What do you think about this five million heist?' Manny chuckled richly. 'God I hope they get away with it. There's always some stupid guy. Who is that guy? Face like a diseased football, comes rushing up, hey bars! Somep'n terrible's happened! Who is that? Myself, I think they're out of the country!'

'I'll tell you in a minute,' David said.

Ha ha, nice one. You cut it in slices – 'Aubergine!' Manny cried. David could not nod or shake his head. On this expedition he had been sold into marriage, the national economy was intact, he achieved very little. A few more slides. The tally boy came rushing back. 'Hey, something terrible's happened – '

'What did I say!' said Manny: 'Lionel Stander!'

The farm at Akeley had been abandoned. 'They found the police had been poking around – that was Ross.' David indicated silence and the lad sat tapping his knees. 'You can talk in front of me,' Manny said, painting on a new mixture of Fuller's Earth and white wine. 'You know who I had in only recently? The chancellor – your friend, Doctor Murray, teach me dancing, in a hurry, hey hey! You wanna know something? They're stopping further education – I said, balls to that Mr Chancellor, it was himself, I said you'd have to shoot me first! Get it? Further education? That's your barber – masseur even better – you going? Okay, I'm sorry. See a witch doctor, doctor.' They came out to the bar.

'Tell me the situation,' David said.

'They've skipped number five, they've gone straight to six – five they can do at seven.' Marchy hoped that didn't mean prison. It was perfectly all right as long as nothing else cropped up. Those policemen were not looking for train robbers, the robbery had not happened then. They were looking for windmills. 'I'm helping them,' Marchy told the steely-eyed wanderer. 'Yes, I know you are. Kathleen told me. She just mentioned it.' David added that, remembering the boy's immature jealousy. The doctor's face was now a problem with women. 'They're going to love it or they're not,' said Marchmont.

The man of many parts watched Marchmont drinking tomato juice at the Big Moon bar. 'You are worried about something, Marchmont. Tell me what it is.' Marchy looked up at the doctor, very worried. 'I'm worried about something, David.' Worried people do not listen. 'You want to talk about it?' The tally boy grimaced, thinks; 'Okay. It's about Elizabeth. Why don't you two live together? She's a lovely person. And what's going to happen to her if Gerry dies of cancer? She's going to be broken up. Can she turn to you again? It's like this girl who committed suicide. This policewoman, Vicky, Vicky Ackroyd, she really thinks I drove her to it. I didn't drive her to it. I mean Albert's customers might have got driven to it – he sold hard, didn't give a fuck where they got the money. I'm not like that – David? Doctor Murray?' Marchmont stood up in the blue romantic light among the dusty Yani Yani leaves. 'He's on the telephone, Mr Marchmont.' This new Mary Quant no dress no knickers no time for strangers Sticks girl stood there, as though baiting a bull. Would she take money? Marchmont now had fifty thousand pounds and a rumoured hundred-thousand from the terrorist clause in the Rio airline's rescued flight 242, now becoming famous.

David came back from the phone. 'You're meeting Reiner Wertzen in the Three Moorhens at Hitchin – eight o'clock. Be sharp.' David put his arm around the worried boy and hugged him, then walked out.

132

'What about your face!' Marchy called. David was whistling *Nuage*, the Ken Colyer arrangement. Soon he would not notice his face. Soon, if he went to visit his African queen he would have to stay in Soweto. In his head he was seeing four-four fret shapes for the number. G-banjo, that is.

Sexton Blake did the great train robbery in the capable script writing hands of Ross's peripatetic old man Malcolm, now in Billericay. A boy phoned the police, following the day's drama in the media, the interviews of the sorters and the slugged driver and a calming law and order statement from official spokesmen which still managed to sound like a continuing Derby Stakes or Michael Bentine getting his own pool results mixed up with his announcing.

'There's a boy on the phone from Clacton, sir – reckons he knows how it was done and where the money is. It's in milk churns. It's standing by the side of the lanes around Towcester in milk churns. He says Sexton Blake bust the same gang a couple of years ago . . .' They gave the call to a woman officer, it being a child. It was Gringo, still at Butlins with Gloria and Rosie, their cabins littered with sex aids. They had tried them all to exhaustion and were now sunbathing. 'I think it's easier straight,' Gringo said. The sun was hot and he had pennies on his eyes. The bright yellow book lay at his side, the title: *Company Of Bandits*. Malcolm had done well with his cover quotes, since the world plaudits for Blake and Tinker and Pedro and Mrs Bardell, the failed Sherlock Holmes of the Amalgamated Press, a world of comics uptilted by the invasion of surrealist poets of the sixties, Mike Moorcock on guitar, Bill Howard Baker mad with foetus of the coming rock explosion now here in his editorial hands, had spread the superlatives around the author's name and left out Blake. MALCOLM MARCHMONT was in big with, one would suppose, a gun in his hand, for author's byline and the pictorial essence of the crime appeared to be one and the same.

'One of the best-known Englishmen in the world' – *Sunday Express*. 'The nearest approach to a 20th Century folklore' – Dorothy L. Sayers. 'Delighted to see Sexton Blake still going strong – and with such aplomb!' – Agatha Christie. His wife Ross came on the phone from Wimbledon, Malcolm then in Hampstead, Horace Fenton in the flat below with his nurses.

'Malcolm – Bill must be round the bend. He hasn't seen this cover but all the quotes except one appear to be about you. Has he paid you?' Ross Woods was then post-Malcolm and post-Horace and in a charming bijou with her cats directly opposite her boss – Bill Baker – in Arterberry Road. He and Irene and Richard and Helga and all the Fentons and Marchmonts were connected children of the sixties, the second coming of the twenties, the great hoedown. They did not know it. Everything blue grass.

Marchmont driving and dreaming. He was not thinking about milk churns. Eric had come into his mind, loved ones of loved ones. David with his painted face, going through hell really, for king and country, never queens unless his own; keeping a straight face. Walking out of Uruguay with Elizabeth and a couple of donkeys, eating human flesh without so much as a gulp, getting held down and painted and then sleeping with pygmies no higher than his balls, then back to the House to report. This was the stuff of the vanishing Faulkners in Mexico or was it – that chap that wrote *Incident at Owl Creek*? Eric Finbow holding a cardboard box behind him, unable to let go of the helm, seeing nothing but early morning mist around him, his motor stopping every time the water intake pipe got blocked with rubbish, unable to hoist the sail, the great heavy mast on its deck-hinge. Marchmont had been aboard it, moored down at Kingston now near Di's dad's flat – Di at the brothel, one of the best. The box he shit in still preserved – New Concentrated Comfort in blue on red. Ambrose Bierce vanished in Old Mexico. When the motor-sailer stopped it turned round and round while he leaned over the side and clawed at the sucked-in rubbish. In his mind Marchmont, while driving his Rover, was concentrating on getting the rubbish away and starting the engine, identifying with Kathleen's man who she called for under anaesthetic. The milk churns went past without being noticed but he stopped the car almost within its own length. The churns were in his mind, his infallible subconscious.

'Those are they!' he said. And he pointed. He was being Sheila Addison the young school teacher who always called him Marchmont. At all times. Wife, wife, wife . . . Marchmont, oh Marchmont. Running up and down the hockey field at Harpenden on Saturday afternoons, where she was bullying off in her capacious white shorts. Now she had gone back

135

to Cambridge. They used to sing, Che Sera, Sera, whatever will be will be, the future looks good to me, che sera, sera.

'Hello – is Chief Inspector Gamble there? This is Marchmont – oh, hello, Vicky. I didn't recognise you. I think I've got something for you – those milk churns – all right, but I can't wait here, I've got a date. There's about ten of them on a platform at the drift, name of the farm, I don't know – and I saw some more further along, the lane that comes down from Icknield to the Three Moorhens. You'll need a low loader, they're probably full of milk! Yes, I made special note of the silver embossed museum tags – that's all right, love. If there's a reward, I'll buy you a din dins somewhere nice.'

Reiner Wertzen sat outside in his Merc with its black windows, to see if Marchmont had been followed. He did not trust him. He was always laughing and making unfathomable remarks. But he needed to see him and to work out a method of getting Marchmont's share away from him afterwards. Murder was not out of the question. They had the gas and to spare. Odourless.

'Hello, Reiner! Is there anyone finer! In the state of Carolina! What'll it be?' Our lad dancing ahead, clapping his hands. But not for long. It was time for another nose bleed. They really should have told him. They ought to trust Marchmont who is not just a song and dance man. It was his idea, after all. His dad had added the milk churns and Gamble had compounded them. They would now stand in among the lovely old farm hardware until next spring when somebody at Slacey Hill might be allocated to give them a good scouring out ready for the dairy section on open day with its concrete cows. A number of people saw this possibility and luckily they were friends of the earth.

Kathleen was at Marchmont's bedside when he came out of his nose bleed. He had been calling for his Rover, the doctor told her, the same doctor she had called for Eric. But this time he knew that her name was not Rover – that had to be his dog.

'It's his car,' she smiled. The doctor, Colombo, raised his hands in the air and walked away from them. Colombo looked like Herbert Lom in *Cianara* with James Mason. Marchmont looked up at her from his pillow. 'Tell me what happened. I've been unconscious all night.' She said, 'You have not been unconscious.' The Irish rose reached over and took off his hospital bed wireless headphones, from the Sisters of Mercy. He had been glued to the interrupted news bulletin that five million pounds had been recovered by the serious crimes squad, the local division of which was headed by Nathan Proud, hidden inside fourteen hundred-gallon antique milk churns. The news had not been interrupted, the bulletin had not been broadcast, the money, so far as the waiting world was concerned, had not been found. By dawn, five men had been shot and two drowned – one jumped from the top of the carillon at Stevenage, Herts. Some were gas and some were snooker players from Gerry's.

'You are the only person that's fireproof, my darling,' Kathy told him. He was the only one who did not know where the five million pounds was to be hidden. Gringo knew. Sexton Blake knew. 'What's going to happen?' Marchy said. 'I want to marry you,' she said. They now had enough to live on. About two million. She told him she had been to see Eric's cousin, Alice Finbow, Albert's widow, Mrs Argyle if you like. 'She wants to come in with her million pools win – Wonderful Things! She loves it, it's like Albert coming true, she said, she did, she did – Albert never came true.' They were laughing together and Marchmont felt a strange affinity with the prototype tally boy. 'He was never allowed to step off the kerb,' Marchy said. Albert's last enterprise had been the reverse steering bicycle. He had bought it because it was cheap. 'It's not cheap when you try to ride it,' the dealer had told him. Oh dear, how appropriate, it was a clown's bike. Within six months Albert was earning a hundred pounds a day with it, three goes to stay on for a quid – a tenner if you won. The Bicycle Rodeo was a winner because it was simple. Nothing could go wrong and there was nobody to pay except one or two winners a year. But the trouble was he went on making bird noises.

'I'm like that,' Marchmont told Kathleen when she was dressing him to come home. He was rich but he would have to keep pushing it. The Alberts were not happy unless they were a bit pressed – Horace, Malcolm, Albert, Marchmont, one day it would be Gringo. Are you having any fun? Whatcha getting out of living? What's the good of what you've got, if you're not, having any fun! 'Are you singing?' she said. He whistled it for her; he was driving his Rover and they were going home.

'Gringo is Greek Anna's son,' Kathleen said. She

was linking with the last thought process. March-mont stopped whistling. 'I hope you're not going to tell me something complicated. I'm a sick man.' It was a nice drive home and later making him a dinner at the brothel with Ruby looking in and Di and Mary wanting to know if he was better, if he had a lot of money, if the five millions had any connection, Kathleen recapped on Anna the Greek. The baby she had by a Vatican priest was Gringo. The story she told Marchmont before he discovered that she was his sister-in-law was true, of course it was. 'Do you know anything about the catacombs?' she asked him. Was it anything like the curry comb, like for horses? Kathleen as a catholic just ploughed on. Zampitini the priest, Gringo's dad, had died in the catacombs under the Vatican, of neglect. The little mother he had been with got out fast but could not call help.

'They are under a vow of silence,' the Irish girl explained.

'I bet she was,' the lad said. He could have said, tough, huh? All the alternatives were always going on in the clown's head. They took precedence over life itself. Marchmont did not know his own rela-tions. He thought Kathleen had picked a funny man on a pole without researching. Everybody knew his depth. There were no wisecracks for it. 'You're worried about something,' he told her the next day. She was worried he had not made any specific request for her hand in marriage, for going to Donegal or Bective Bridge or talking to hers and Ruby's brothers, the bhoys. About some things he was too much like Albert. Lunch time one o'clock, Friday, August seventeen, Doctor David Murray came in with a bottle of light wine and some oysters done up in ice. They sat and enjoyed themselves – five dozen oysters, two bottles. His information was that the officers of the Slacey Collection of Agricultural Machinery wanted to thank him for spotting their milk churns.

'They found the money,' David told them, to pre-empt what lay heavy in their faces. 'They've burnt it. They thought it was rubbish – paper. A chap called Eagles or some such. He tested them with his boot – they didn't ring properly. They didn't like to put their arms in, you know, rats or shit or whatever. Eagles poured some white spirit in – they use a lot of this white spirit for restoring the implements. I managed to buy two off him – before they were burnt.' The WHO man tipped a package out of his Budgen plastic carrier, together with some good size wet herrings which he had brought from the oyster shop. 'There's a million pounds in there – it's yours, Claude. Never talk about it, share it as you will. Don't say, what about you.' His face was different; he had coloured in the white stripes to match the purple ones. He had also changed his passport to black.

'We're getting married,' Kathleen told David.

'Halloween,' said Marchmont. He was thinking, only another million! That wouldn't go anywhere. Physically, the package weighed twenty pounds *avoir du pois*. They went on swallowing oysters. Ruby and the girls came in with bottles, two men, Chelsea Ted from Gerry's. Burnt or not, there had been enough ackers to pay everybody something and the casualties were exaggerated. Not much higher than usual.

Reiner had been sent to the Seychelles for unspecified action, Gerry Chapman had been re-diagnosed, less fatally. The most important thing for Marchmont happened in Chesham. It is in Buckinghamshire. Two things happened within the same hour. A girl in front of him at the cashout lost her car keys. He was feeling bored and unhappy. He had got himself some of those figs with white sugar coating and was looking forward to driving back to Hitchin and eating them en route. He was disappointed that being a millionaire had not altered this as a high point. Two weeks ago he had done this, when he only had about twenty-thousand. Last year on ten pounds dole money the figs had topped the week for him. He was wanting to summon the courage to pop one in his mouth while still in the queue, before they were paid for, a mad surge of adrenalin – then all at once the raincoated lady in front clapped her hands in her pockets and cried: 'Oh, my God! My keys! My car keys!'

It was a dreadful predicament. She had two small children and an enormous trolley of food. Like she was buying for a hostel – or a zoo. He had counted twenty-three tins of cat food. The woman on cashout, a Chinese or Japanese woman with a large flat face, like a pizza, he thought, had paged the lost keys on the store loudspeakers and pretty soon, by the time the hotel full of food had been cashed through, a shop manager, ginger, freckles, protruding teeth, came dangling them to her. Marchy felt irritated with him, but then bucked up when they were the wrong ones.

'Is there a phone? I'll have to phone my husband.

Trouble is, he said he was going out – he has an appointment with his bookmaker.' She looked full into Marchmont's eyes, as if pleading for help. She said, 'I've seen your picture in the paper – you're Claude Marchmont. You stopped that jet getting blown up.'

'That wasn't in the paper, was it?'

'Next please,' the cashout Nip told them.

'Look,' Marchmont took the young mum's arm. 'I'll run you home. I've got a lovely Rover outside, doing nothing – come on, kids, let's get this loaded.'

'You are kind,' she said.

The whole day was transformed.

'I'm going to buy some Boots,' he told her. She was sitting next to him like a wife, the kids, one little girl and one little boy, hanging their elbows over the backs of the seats. 'What size do you take?' she asked. Her name was Jody and she was a food inspector. He explained he was going to buy up Boots the chemists, to get a good ready-made chain of shops. She fell silent and looked worried. He worked it out that it must sound like bullshit. Being a millionaire would not be easy, socially.

Her voice became cold. 'It's the next turning – thank you, so much.' I've really fucked it, he thought. Then it changed again. Came his way. Her husband had not gone to his bookie, her husband was in bed with her sister, who was staying with them. Ten minutes later both their lives had changed, he was driving fast after her, she was running, alone, without the children, without the shopping, just running in the middle of the road – it took a mile to get in front of her and cut her off. By that time they were out of town on the High Wycombe hill.

'Come on, in you get, Hilary.'

'Jody,' she said.

She cried in his arms in the front seat for a long time. And then he kissed her. A long kiss. He realised that he could do anything with her. Anybody could this afternoon, though you would have to work fast. 'Where shall we go?' she asked him, wetly.

'Leave it to me. I'll buy a hotel.'

She suddenly believed in him again. Nice move. One more makes three. They climbed the mountain together, the magic mountain, needing each other, excited at new love. There was dinner at the Marlow Lodge, dancing at a river club at Henley, chats with strangers, a honeymoon. At the sobering hour of three o'clock in the morning, the Gatsby waltz, Jody sat up in bed. She said, 'You're not asleep, are you?' He was not asleep. She said, 'You were crying.' He said, 'So were you.' She kissed him and then it was over. They went home.

'You were late, dear,' said the Irish rose.

Marchmont was doing the pancakes. 'Try this.' She liked it. He kissed her forehead. 'I want to marry you.' There should be a song, you have to find out. By sleeping with somebody else . . . They bought the ring in Hitchin and he went to buy some champagne for luncheon. In the liquor store he was about to ask for it but then didn't. 'Have you got half a bottle of Scotch? Thanks.' He got some dry ginger and some beer. At the fraud squad office later in the morning, Charlie Gamble said to Vicky Ackroyd, 'You ought to change that toothpaste – it's full of chlorophyll.' She

143

smiled, then lost the smile and remembered the moment in the off-licence. When he was going to buy champagne or a whole bottle of scotch and then didn't. She decided to close the case. Marchmont, her suspect, chummy, had decided to open it. Vicky stinking up his heels, worried him. If he was going to wear Albert Argyle's shoes and start getting married, he wanted to be a virgin and he could afford it now.

The flying doctor came back from Billericay, from Hillingdon, from Rome and from Jersey, finally reporting back to Finbow's in Bute Street. Jen was coming out with her five children and their new boots, all kissed by Uncle Claude.

'Massa Marchmont! Dare's a nigger in de shop!' This is Gringo. 'Get rid of that boy,' David said. Marchmont pushed the lad into the ladies dresses – 'Get in there or he'll eat you!' And to his visitor, the man with the blue-black complexion, he offered a brief hug. They left the shop like a dancing couple doing a double chassée. 'Kathleen's gone to America with Gerry Chapman,' Gloria told her staff, pre-empting Marchmont's lunch at the George.

'Philadelphia,' spoke the oddly-coloured face of the government emissary, man about the world, known in the Upper Chamber as The Walker. He kept sending Lord Taylor home. It was his job at home base, as occupational therapist to the quick and the slumbering. David Murray in the slurry, he called it when carving his stiltons at Petsoe End. Eddie Condon was his mentor. Banjo, that is.

'Not Philadelph – I – A?' said the tally boy, rolling

his eyes and spreading his palms guess who – 'Al Jolson,' his friend said, 'but in very bad taste until I get my face back.' A well known dermatologist in Camden was whitening pop singers. 'What does human flesh taste like?' said Marchmont, changing the subject in his jokey way. 'Not like this,' David said. This was the George's tasty version of French haricot lamb. 'More like goat.'

'That figures.' Slow nodding, nod, nod, Kathleen, Ruby, informed affirmative of the rock and the roll. In Philadelphia there was a surgeon specialist for Gerry Chapman's throat cancer. 'We only got to him through the Kennedys' good will – Kathleen knows Jack Kennedy and the clan.' David spotted the shadow on the young man's chewing jaws. 'It's not Chappaquiddick it's the Battle of Bective Bridge – he came over.'

'I remember – to see his ancestral Kennedy village. I've got an estate agent girl in Newport Pagnell, a beautiful Kennedy. I carried her poles. So it's the IRA, then? Secret meetings between the President and Cyril Cusack? Peter Sellars in the spit and sawdust looking for the jelly and getting slugged? I'm with you. Kathleen the heroine blowing up cows to rescue her soldier boy – or was that Ruby Mahallahan?' Without stopping his eating, the doctor reached into his green German shirt pocket, moleskin that is, and handed the boy a photostat letter which Marchmont turned in his hand, sniffed and rejected as phony – you could see faint ruled lines of the original and the outline of a perforated torn edge, as ripped from a notebook. It was a xerox, a photocopy, David explained, it was American and Rank at Pinewood.

'It's from Midge Corby to Albert Argyle and Horace gave it to me on Sunday in St Helier – we went through Albert's stuff together. Horace is sending you Albert's scout badge – still got your badge, have you? Remember, Cedric the school teacher on the petrol pumps in the evenings to keep up with his wife's account with Albert? From Horace, one gets these intimacies – it's still a continuing saga.'

'Now he's marrying it?'

'No, he's not. With Tres it's old mates – whatever it was in the books. Tres is independent, she has a pretty daughter, a good business and Jersey credibility – that means money without wealth. Horace and Alice Finbow may get married, though they are both swiftly falling in love with the freedoms, aren't we all – '

'When did you see Alice?'

'Last night. She's working for Middlesex County Council.'

'Her dad was a tax man – is she still Mrs Argyle?'

'Yep – but as a librarian it's not a good name.'

Two slowly nodding heads over the haricot lamb. Letter neatly typed, copy of:

My Dear Man – Are you okay? Loved your dyeing the Thames red! Is that a Thunderbirds promotion for Gerry Anderson? I remember you opened the real life wild park or some such similar at Woburn with your FAB 1! I nearly caught up with you and your procession at Tenterden – you had gone with the police and an ambulance. It sounded like Belfast over again with the mayor and corporation out. Something caught fire at Tenterden? I still live nearby you know! It wasn't Di, was it? Lady Penelope? Give her my love – tell her I saw you first at East Heath Road, the menagerie. I have been fastening onto making money and so far succeeded only with direct method – temping, as I am this week (today is Fri) in Amnesty International which has been a rare gift – a joy to be in! Other temp assignments being probably awful, and for intrinsic reasons as well I am hoping I dare busk again. Chickened out so far. Do you want to join me? Miss your yodeling and Sylvia's cello drifting up through that awful rusty bog window at East Heath, the pigeons! Will write more to the point (some point or other) soon. Just send love, meanwhile . . .

Hope all goes okay, Albert (can you still pick me up?) –

love:
Midge X X X

'Would you like the rice pudding?'
'Marchmont?'
'Hm?'
The whole letter had taken him closer into his prototype's life than even Kathleen or Horace or Malcolm his dad. The whole letter had the status that only lovers have for each other as persons. The trouble was, Marchmont did not know the writer. She was not a part of his briefing.
'It's Midge Hammond,' Murray explained.
'Midge Hammond?' The pole squatter's long nose and eyebrows stopped working, the charm solidified. This expresses rank disbelief. Midge Hammond

belonged in the penny-pinching, soul destroying, body-giving world of the tally boys, the brass tongs and brush and shovel of life's rich pattern. This letter-writer would never commit suicide. In his hands was the real Midge, not the lady her mourners mourned or WPC Ackroyd had sworn to revenge in the name of woman. David saw that it had sunk in and they both sat slowly nodding their heads like rear window ducks over their rice pudding. Whoever heard of putting rice in a pudding, it seemed to say.

13

Marchmont dressed for golf strode into Clophill Manor and across to the desk, midday Saturday, busy busy time. The desk girl had seen him parking the white Rover and had already dialled out, got a hurried call completed by the time he reached her, hung up, swung a gun from under the desk so that only he could see it, though others were around, waiting for attention, waiting for nothing.

'Before you say anything, Marchmont, I'm not the kind of an whore – a whore, rather – who rolls guys.' Marchmont did a Jack Benny, which is closing his lips together even though tortured. 'Right. Then listen, Marchy, telephone Lady Lewis on her home number at Chicheley Hall and talk to me afterwards at the members' bar.' She turned to the Chief Constable of the county, Henry Wannamaker, standing in work-out briefs and slippers and mopping his neck. 'Take the next booth, sir,' she said. She gave him Marchmont's booth telephone number and he went for it, dancing a little and moving his shoulders, only a pace behind the hero.

In his kiosk Marchmont dialled and got a voice and then another voice, recognisable. 'Lady Lewis?' 'Is that Mr Marchmont? I'm Hilda – nice to talk to you. You did a wonderful job in Brazil – so many people owe you their lives. I've had many inquiries from all over the world, asking for your address – I withhold it and promise to tell you and later on make an announcement at the presentation. You know the airline has paid a quarter million dollars not pounds into your Swiss account – I have a number and code but will not reveal it on an open line – Mr Marchmont? Claude!' Henry Wannamaker popped round from the next booth and found him on the floor, Kattery came running from the desk with tissues and water in a beaker. Her real name was Kattery Klaus, a poet from Toronto filling in with an adrenalin job with the Danger Agency.

'His nose is bleeding,' said Wannamaker.

'Yes, I know.' She picked up the tiny voice of Lady Lewis and told it she would call back. 'Listen,' Wannamaker was breathing into Marchy's mouth, as if resuscitating him, 'We want the diamonds and we want your Swiss account code number and teletex cash transfer authority – and where is Gerry's boat?'

'Where am I?' Marchmont asked, trying to sit up.

The American USAAF first-aid team came trotting up and got him away on a stretcher. One of the trotters had a blue-black face and Marchy muttered his thanks. Kattery was secretly pleased. 'Can I help you, Mr Wannamaker? I'm sure he'll come back. His Irish calls are coming here – mostly ladies. He organises charities for deserving causes – oh – ' The Chief Constable placed his hand over her mouth for a moment. 'Do you play squash?' Kattery shook her pretty head and then watched the big man shuffling back to the games area, shadow boxing whoever was fucking him up.

'Is this your Browning 22?'

The security guard was the same little man who had been a Kathleen watcher and had got himself blown up with Marchmont's little blue Vauxhall and lost his secret cigarette papers. Kattery took the gun and absently hung it on a keys rack. It was in her mind to initiate something. She had met Murray in Paris while he was still white and had come back with him to London for something unspecified, which turned out to be roughly true and not unenjoyable. The colour change after Brazil she could never quite accept as disguise. In the night he was making Aranguana pygmy noises and beating tom toms. Her father was Chancellor of the Toronto City and State Exchequer. She had got a poem out of it and sent to them.

> Tucca wanta toffeehunter
> Gotta lotta mukinsted,
> Kattery has joined the junta
> Jelly babies blue this year.

'Is Mr Marchmont here?' This was the police, WPC Victoria Ackroyd, with a warrant for Marchy's arrest. Information had been received to rekindle her love for him. She had changed her toothpaste and was no longer hampered by Gamble – she had left fraud. This was the sheriff in New York time. She looked around as Kattery wrote down the address of the US hospital – down there a mile and second on the left. 'You've got a gun hanging up there – is it loaded?'

Kattery got it and fired it into the roof. 'Yes, miss! Jesus!' She handed it over, shrugged her apology to the vestibule, now coming to life with mini-dressed girls from the village, a band bringing in instruments for the Plaza tea-dance, tea for two and I'm young and healthy, and you've got charm – 'balls', the girls sang it. There was a megaphone and a Rudy Vallee. 'It belongs to the Chief Constable,' Kattery explained about the gun. 'Attaturk – not Attaturk, Wanna-maker.' Attaturk, Vicky preferred. She had dis-covered new evidence, brought to her voluntarily, since Vicky after the toothpaste incident had aban-doned the Finbow corruption vendetta with its sex aid overtones; new evidence that Marchmont was the father of Pilgrim Hammond, Midge's middle boy. Discovered not by blood test or genetics or similarity, but by Midge having told her husband. This had been the concealed portion of bitterness and self-hate. She told him the night he pissed in the ward-robe. The crusading policewoman decided to walk the mile and sort out her true allegiances.

'Every story is a song, every song is a painting, every painting is a piece of music, that's what Horace says and thinks and does – not so Malcolm, my dad. People say, Mal and Horry seem the same guy, the same age, the same history in books and stories and television – Mal on *Dixon*, Horry on *The Informer*, Mal on *Market in Honey Lane*, a dozen more, Mal and Horace and Bob Holmes and Richard Harris and Louis Marks and Charles Wood cornering the

152

market, good editors sitting atop them, Eric Maschwitz and Pat Alexander (Eric wrote *The Berkeley Square Nightingale* and *Goodnight Vienna*, you know – how d'you do, this is Horace Spurgeon Fenton) Donald Bull finished with Escapers Club and coming up for the never-ending forgotten Doctor somebody's thingme. It's your books, Horace! said Donald Bull, pulling the old rascal – who started that? – out of his caravan.'

'Without your caravan you are nothing,' Louis Marks told him. Hampstead was full of old writers.

'That's very interesting, Mr Marchmont, but it doesn't help Mr Hammond or the children – I want Midge Hammond's accounts, what she bought, what she paid, what she didn't pay and how you took her arrears – and made her pregnant. I have advised Mr Hammond to sue you on a private prosecution.' They were not in the Chicksands hospital but in the garden of the PX store and canteen. They were not unwatched. It took forty-eight hours to get de-briefed from the early warning red-button Russia-watching gasometer. Nobody went unobserved.

'Do you hate me?' Marchmont asked her. His nose had cotton wool in it and his head was bandaged because his rescuer, Wannamaker, old Henry the top cop had managed to kick it. The young policewoman had wound down with her accusations. She rather liked him. She breathed hard for a moment, then said, 'I think you're rotten.' He thrust the girl's letter at her. It was like one of his mother's westerns and he knew every last move. 'Then read this!' When Marchy was five he wandered from Ross to Mal and back to Ross, tap tap tap. 'Are you writing another

153

nobble?' It never seemed to pay the landowners and they were always getting cut off at the gas.

'I don't understand this,' Vicky the policewoman said. 'Who's Midge? How can you dye the river Thames red? Is this a script?' John Wayne walked past and Marchmont had a double-take. 'That's John Wayne!' he pointed. Stars often visited US bases but nobody ever knew it at the end of the drive, in England. 'This is not from Midge Hammond,' the WPC said.

'Yes, it is. Her name was Corby, her father was a doctor in London, Connaught Square near Marble Arch. I had to go wee-wees down his basement steps one night – she was Jay Lewis's secretary and played in a skiffle group. That's where she met Hammond, he was Hammy Hammond the wiffle skiz, top of the broomstick, dooma dooma doom – without it he was a labourer. That's how it happens, officer. She wasn't conned by Albert Argyle, she loved him. Horace did a movie with Jay Lewis and that's how Albert met her – Albert was always hanging around with the Fentons and the Marchmonts. If she hadn't died she wouldn't have stayed with Hammond – not with the kids growing up. My son Pilgrim.' Is love a secret shy and cold anadyomene, silver-gold?

Victoria placed her hand on his hand. He was a dad and mummy was not here. They worked it out when the letter was written and when she died and when Albert died and who might die next or get blown up. 'She worked for Amnesty International,' Marchmont said. 'That's dangerous.' They had more coffee and watched John Wayne go past the other way, giving each other a little wave. 'This train

154

robbery,' the policewoman said, as though reminded by the Hollywood master of train robberies. 'There's more behind that than local crooks.' Marchmont gave it the slow nod. She read his mind. It was not on her legs any more. She said: 'You can go and talk to Mr Hammond about the boy – he'll be all right. When you get married perhaps you can share him – I was told you were getting married.'

'Is that what started this? The handcuffs?'

He leaned forward and she rested her head against him. There is no real answer. 'Oh, isn't the world full, of wonderful things,' she sang, softly. Marchmont sat apart and looked at her. She smiled at him, sadly and went on singing, softly. 'The skies blue, deep, the waves that keep on turning – The moonlight and then, the morning born again . . . The promise of love, soon, lending me wings – oh, isn't the world full, of wonderful things, wonderful things . . . ?' They kissed for a fade-out without fading out – Americans standing nearby were swaying and singing oooo, oooo, oooo, oooo. John Wayne came back. 'How did you know about that Wonderful Things?' asked the tally boy. He thought it was one of his brightest ideas, the perfect love shop, but she told him it was a song already. A movie and a song, Frankie Vaughan and Jean Dawnay starred with producer Anna Neagle and director Herbert Wilcox and his daily red carnation. Dear old Wilfred Hyde-White was daddy, a Liberty Store millionaire.

'Would you marry someone like me?' Victoria asked Marchmont.

'I was just thinking about that,' he said. 'While you

were singing. Horace stuck with Evelyn all her life because they sang together in the thirties. They saw every Bing Crosby movie and sat by the river and sang them, the songs, Love in Bloom – '

'Can it be the trees, that fills the breeze, with rare and magic perfume – ' the policewoman started and he stopped her, 'Okay, okay, I get it – I tell you what, I'll think about it. If Kathleen's not back from America by Halloween, ask me again.'

'I like little boys,' she said. 'Pilgrim's like you!'

Unworthy though it was, he wondered if she knew about his wealth and his diamonds and the Swiss coded bank account organised by Red Cross International. Only in America could this happen, in a movie with the Duke walking by and a policewoman singing love songs with her legs open and hoping to get cast.

'I wish I could get out of this uniform,' she said, as if capturing his glance. 'Do this – action – ' he unzipped her blouse and stopped her protest. 'This is a movie – first we find a field, Anna Magnani in *Rice*?' They had to walk back, both their cars were at the squash club. 'I could raise a police car,' she offered. Let me do the raising, was in his head, but he waited for something better, one of the three smart answers.

Nobody walked the busy road between the Air Force base and Clophill Manor. William Saroyan once walked the lovers' path to see how the corn was making out. Today it seemed ten feet high, fiercely hot and brown and with islands of poppies and the purple rosebay willow herb. Voices out of sight. I have promised Gerry that I will not be unfaithful to

Kathleen. Yes, I know that and respect you for it. But still, I want you. And you've got the handcuffs, bonny lass. It's not handcuffs, Marchy – it's getting nailed to the floor. I am the only living person who picked up the telephone and took your call about the milk churns. Think about it.

Marchmont yielded; he had made no mistake with WPC Ackroyd. She came up to all her duties.

14

The car park at the manor had an ominous neglect of human presence about it. Marchmont felt that it had been booby-trapped.

'Is that your police patrol car?' he asked Victoria.

'Yes. What's happened to it!'

Marchy stopped her from moving. The police car had had its wheel clamped to prevent it getting taken away. Marchy and the young lady constable stared at each other, filled with guilt. Filled with guilt! Nothing less that this unheard-of officialdom had been in their guts since fucking each other.

'This is *The Last Detail* again,' Marchy said, nodding, nodding. 'Jack Nicholson?' His Rover was also clamped. Slowly they searched the big rough, tatty, body-builders' night-shagging 1963 America in bed with England car park for some sign that others were guilty, God waiting. Forget it. Then a loud electric roar of silence was switched on and a voice filled with hate and menace called:

OFFICER CRUMPET!

'Oh, my God!' she said.

Marchmont encircled her with his arm. 'Don't worry. They have no proof.'

'But supposing they search us? I forgot to put my knickers on!'

'Here you are – I've got them, put 'em on. They can't see us. That's control talking. They think we're Russian,' he added, grasping for a ray of hope. It was going to be vastly different in the distant future when the Russians won, simply by backing out. The whole planet balanced on Atlas's head and no way of putting it down. The big early-warning gasometer burning while the reds slept under beds. Power stations blew up.

IF YOU HAVE FIREARMS THROW THEM ON THE GROUND AND COME TO THE LOCKER ROOM WITH YOUR HANDS ON YOUR HEADS!

'That's Rod Steiger!' Marchmont exclaimed.

'Put your hands on your heads!' said the girl.

'I've only got one fucking head – stop panicking. This is a gag. Somebody tailed us to the field! It's your boy friend, Charlie Gamble.'

'I'm not with him now, I'm not in fraud – everything's changed in the force. I'm going to be mounted.'

'I pass,' said Marchy. He had a choice of three.

They were now obeying orders and walking towards the squash club, but Marchy rebelled. 'Fuck 'em,' he said. The WPC faced him, lowered her hands. They were not going to be shot dead by anybody. Marchmont shouted:

PUT YOUR FINGER UP YOUR BUM AND PISS OFF!

Somewhere near, a little man holding a loud-hailer

got out of his Vauxhall 14. It was the detective who had started by keeping Kathleen's record of copulations and then got blown up by the IRA in mistake for Ruby Hanrahan. 'Hello,' he said. He was not smiling but he looked pleased.

'Was that you?' Marchy asked him.

'It was! Yes, it was! Though I haven't followed you or anything, this afternoon. It's a lovely day, though. I am Detective Superintendent Bloggs. I have to ask you a few questions. It's about the train robbery at Salcey Forest. You don't have to answer me, but anything you say may be noted and used in a court of law. As the young lady knows. We can get a pot of tea here – the girl's name is Kattery Klaus. She works for the syndicate and has been cleared by the Foreign Office – as a Canadian national working for The Danger Agency. That's like Alfred Marks Bureau or Manpower – yes, sir?'

'Will you shut up?' Marchmont said.

It had dawned on both the lad and his lover that they were dealing with a lunatic, a detective-story bookworm. A film buff. Maybe a writer. 'Do your Rod Steiger voice again – it's from *The Heat Of The Night*.'

'Oh yes, yes.' Bloggs cleared his throat and uttered his menacing warnings, but forgot to switch on the loud-hailer. It sounded silly. He took a gun out of his pocket instead.

'That's not allowed!' Vicky told him.

'It is if you have a gun,' said the detective. 'Or if I have reason – '

'All right, all right,' Vicky said. 'Let's go and have this tea.' They all turned to the locker room entrance

160

where several men, partially dressed, had gathered, disturbed by unusual activity; it was neither afternoon nor bar time yet. A car now came in – CID, Gamble driving. His expression said to Vicky, are you all right? Her expression said yes. He did not join them yet. The fake detective took them into tea.

'It's over here, Superintendent,' said Kattery Klaus, now superbly dressed for skiing. She seemed to know the little man very well, which depressed them both, fears returning. Bloggs detected this and tried to disarm them. 'I don't want to intrude into your private life.'

'If you said that with Gerry Chapman around, I would be intruded to death,' Marchmont told him. He was not supposed to have a private life.

Bloggs smiled. 'Gerry's not all bad. He puts Tipp-ex on spiders' legs.' Marchmont fell silent and they all drank tea, as if in truce or despair. Bloggs was genuine; when some people are genuine it's frightening. Bloggs wanted to know where Claude Marchmont was on the night of August 27. He had got the wrong date.

'I was in Billericay with my father.'

'That's right.' The superintendent from Special Branch, which is the truth about him, checked his little notebook, the one Marchy had returned to his pocket while Bloggs was unconscious.

'He was there the whole day,' Vicky told her superior officer. 'I put it in my report.'

'Yes – ' now in his bright smile one saw the reason for his presence: anything the WPC had reported – although Bloggs had thoughtfully left his binoculars in his Vauxhall 14 – was now to be checked. Luckily

161

the references were substantial: 'There was a cricket match, a girl in a mini-dress with an ice cream, a police girl from St Osyth who waved to him – to you, that is.'

'She was eating an orange,' Marchy remembered, noddingly.

'But how do we know it was the day following the five million pounds TPO robbery?' asked Bloggs.

'Not many people eat oranges,' said Marchy.

WPC Ackroyd quietly pressed his arm. Splendid, she thought. There is something idiotically universal in a Pinnochio, give a little whistle. They don't know right from wrong. Everything that happens to them seems separate. There is no continuity. Marchmont had remembered Kathleen shooting this chap. 'How's your business going, sir?' he asked, putting his little book away as if for good, having wiped tea off the cover. Marchy did not have to reply, he knew that anyway but also, Gamble entered the refreshment room and hurried over, greeting Bloggs as Percy. They got him a chair and a cup and chatted weather, traffic, police talk. You heard about O'Brien? And so on.

'Are you two getting married then?' Vicky's inspector asked them, and to Percy Bloggs: 'This is why she came chasing up here!' Laughter. 'They all do it!' Our heroes were not doing it, however. It was just a nice summer afternoon at Clophill. 'I've got to be off,' said our ubiquitous dwarf, catching sight of somebody outside.

'Check your car for bombs,' he warned his colleagues as he went out. Will do, ta ta, see you. Bloggs went away a few steps then swung round, as in the movie, fired a question at Charlie Gamble.

'What were you doing on the night of the twenty-seventh, Charlie?'

'I don't know.'

'Ah yes, that's right. Are you on plain clothes duty then?'

'No – I've left the force, I'm going to Canada. I've been left a farm in Calgary. An old aunt. Talk to the Chief Constable – Wannamaker.'

'No, that's all right – we've nearly finished the inquiry now, thank God. Good luck, in case I don't see you, Charlie . . .'

When he'd gone out they remained silent, Marchy and the uniformed police girl, watching him appear in the car park and go to his Vauxhall 14, where he opened a door and took out binoculars and scanned distant places, rotating. Now Kattery Klaus was also watching from her cash counter. The Special Branch man put his binoculars away and went down on his knees on the gravel and inspected the chassis for limpet bombs.

When he drove away he gave them a toot. He had not unclamped their wheels.

'I'm glad I'm out of it,' Charlie said.

Marchmont and WPC Ackroyd nodding. Charlie was quietly laughing, as if glad of the chance. 'Bloggy's a comedian,' he explained. Marchmont was relieved. He got up from the table and left Vicky and Charlie together, which they needed. The old crew.

'Kattery!'

She came to him, cautiously smiling. 'You look like Lee Remick,' he told her. 'Can you give us a room?

163

We need a bath and a change of clobber. How's David?' This was in case she had forgotten their mutual friends. 'How about his face!' she said. Then she said. 'It's starting to fade around here.' She was touching her nipples and stopped it. She said, 'He rang yesterday from the House of Commons. About bonfire night. Yes, I know it's the summer still, but David is fanatical about everybody in his life around his bonfire on the fifth of November – I've seen you there!' He knew she was trying and failing to cover the nipples slip and then she confessed it:

'For heaven's sake, Claude, don't let your dad write anything more about me in his books! My family read him! I was in one of his short stories on Radio Three – *The Moment of the Flying Fish*. It was in the interval of the Buddy Rich jazz concert, a story about this place, Chicksands, that five-minute alert they had in March? I was the cause of that – the guy on the red button was trying to blow the world up because I wouldn't sleep with him!'

'I would do that,' Marchmont promised her. She was talking about Horace Spurgeon Fenton, not Malcolm; the confusion was much. Sometimes Horace wrote under the name Trevor for what he called his entertainments. Kattery sorted out a room with bathroom and gave him the keys. He looked up at the number. 'This was our room!'

'Tell Horace to change my name.'

Claude held her hand for a moment, on the counter. She said: 'He's got the Queen blowing up the Channel Tunnel in his new book! They build this tunnel under the sea from Calais to Dover and it's been plastered with odourless Semtex – dog – proof!

164

What the IRA use. The Queen thinks she's cutting a ribbon!'

'I remember!' said Marchmont. 'He tries his stuff on the kids at Christmas.'

'It's set about thirty years in the future – nineteen ninety, something like that. The Royal Train is going to be the first thing to cross – it's called the Paris Belle. Of course, it doesn't get there. And there's no loss of life. The tunnel is empty.'

'He never kills innocent bystanders, old Horace.'

'Neat! Even the Queen is surprised! The Channel goes up right across twenty miles, like God waiting! For the Israelites! Then he gets the Brits out of Ireland! Your government has to go to Sinn Fein to ask them to take responsibility for blowing up the tunnel, and that's their condition! To get Queen Elizabeth off the hook! Clever, isn't it.'

'I haven't read it all yet. I prefer Paul Theroux. Who actually sabotaged the tunnel, then? All that Semtex. That was the Russians. They make that stuff in Czechoslovakia – or Vladivostok, as Albert would say about silk worms. His doorstep documentaries.'

'It was the ferries,' said Kattery. 'They paid for it. Sealink and P & O. They had been refused shares in Eurotunnel. They call everything Euro in the nineties – well, Horace does. He comes here you know.'

That line stood on its own, as if stopped. Marchmont was sensitive enough to remain quiet. Inspector Gamble called a goodbye and waved, Vicky went with him to the door and kissed him and stood long enough to see him go. She was crying and wiped her nose on her hand. Marchy was kind.

'I've got a room, love, if you want to clean up.'

There was a feeling of familiarity and love between the three people that goes unexplained. Unexplainable. Gamble's father was having a serious affair with Gamble's wife. Charlie did not want to hurt either of them and so had been trying to lose his job or his driving licence to make an excuse to move to Canada – and separate the couple. Maybe come back for the old man's funeral. But these things did not come to pass.

'Now Charlie's got the money to go and she won't go with him – she wants to stay with Jack.' They were in bed now at the manor, and joined. Wife, wife, wife. 'Charlie wants me to go to Canada with him . . .'

There had been a share-out. The big job, the crime of not the century but perhaps the decade, the frothy sixties, with the sobering death of a President just weeks ahead, this money crime had become irreversible. They could not put it back.

'I've got a horse!' Vicky said. 'My own horse! I call it Charlie. The Foreign Office handled the money, you know. Your friend David Murray. Did you get anything?'

'I've got two million.'

'Well, that's not bad – it was your original idea, wasn't it?' She made the Great Train Robbery sound like song-writing.

Kattery came in later with a selection of nice clothes, skiing, dancing, hiking, sensible. 'I'll be at the bar, you guys!' Horace always meant to change her name but could never quite bring himself to do it or to call her something fictional. At the bar, the Canadian girl who looks more like Natalie Wood

166

than Lee Remick, what with the Indian name, said to the lad, 'Did I hear you mention you have kazookas? I thought so. Ross has been on three times.'

'Look after your mother,' said Victoria, everybody nodding. 'This time we are spelling Kateri as Kattery – her dad's idea.'

Happy endings. As he grew older, into the seventies and then into the eighties, of the century, that is, there were several moments in this history of the sixties that Claude Marchmont would remember, often to some new stranger. His life changed as his money turned into different things and places and people. It had been a night at Gerry's with all the actors and the Elstree girls and Mario Zampi was there slumming with the quota quickies and his knowledgeable son Giulio and above all Elizabeth and Chelsea Ted and Frank Searle the B-picture man and the strong memory of Albert Argyle, for Helga had turned up from Hamburg, alive. It was dark and the snow was inches deep and feet deep and Marchmont was piggy-backing Kathleen across the drive and into the trees, noisily. A window slid up and Gerry Chapman's voice, healthy again and sounding like a Tannoy, crackled out: 'Please fuck off home, Marchy, some of us want to go to bed!' Kenneth More was getting into his car with Angela.

One day, chased by the police and with a load of Wonderful Things in the boot of his Rover, Marchmont tyre-squealed to stop and the wagon did the same and PC Sid Nation shouted and stuck up his fingers: 'Up your pipe, Marchy!'

'Up yours, mate!'

167

They drove on to their country estate, Kathleen pregnant. 'You've been accepted,' she said. Claude rested his hand on her tum – soon to be called Oliver or Emma. Whispering Paul McDowell and his Temperance Seven were doowackadoowackadoing *Pasadena* on the Pye.